BRENT LIBRARIES

Please return/renew this item
by the last date shown.
Books may also be renewed by
phone or online.
Tel: 0333 370 4700
On-line www.brent.gov.uk/libraryservice

WORLD CUP FEVER

BOB CATTELL

Illustrations by
David Kearney

RED FOX

A RED FOX BOOK 978 0 099 46141 8

First published in Great Britain by Julia MacRae and Red Fox,
imprints of Random House Children's Publishers UK

Julia MacRae edition published 1995
Red Fox edition published 1995
Reissued 2001, 2007

16

Text Copyright © Bob Cattell, 1995
Illustrations Copyright © David Kearney, 1995

Score sheets reproduced with kind permission of David Thomas
© Thomas Scorebooks 1985

Set in Sabon

Red Fox Books are published by Random House Children's Publishers UK
61–63 Uxbridge Road, London W5 5SA,
a division of The Random House Group Ltd,

Addresses for companies within
The Random House Group Limited can be found at:
www.randomhouse.co.uk/offices.htm

THE RANDOM HOUSE GROUP Limited Reg. No. 954009

www.**randomhousechildrens**.co.uk

A CIP catalogue record for this book is available from the British Library.

Penguin ... for
our busi... om

Printe... c

Contents

Chapter One

We weren't even half way through the summer holidays and Glory Gardens had run out of fixtures. Of course, we'd won the Under 13s League in June, but since then we'd just played a few friendlies including another brilliant last-ball victory over Wyckham Wanderers, our deadliest enemy. Now we had no more cricket for the rest of the season.

"I can't see much point in practising when we haven't got anything to practise for," said Jacky. We were changing after Saturday morning Nets and, to be honest, it hadn't been a brilliant session.

"It's a complete waste of time," said Clive who's never been a big fan of net practice and doesn't miss a chance to moan about it.

I love Nets – for me Saturday mornings are the highlight of the week. But even I had to admit it isn't the same if we aren't playing any proper games.

"I suppose we could arrange some more friendlies?" suggested Erica.

"No, we want a competition," said Cal. "A knock-out cup or a tournament or something."

Cal was right. I decided to talk to Kiddo about it after the practice session.

One of the problems about Glory Gardens now is that Azzie, Clive, Marty and I are playing regularly for the County Under 13s Colts. So the four of us have had plenty of games (played 7, won 4, drawn 2, lost 1), but the rest of the team haven't and that's why some of them are getting fed up.

Anyway, it's time I introduced the team properly. I'm Hooker Knight, the captain of Glory Gardens Cricket Club, winners of the North and East County League and the 'best team in the universe' if you believe Frankie Allen. That's us in the picture.

I'm in the middle of the front row with the cricket bat. Cal is the tall one leaning over at the back – he's my best friend. He lives next door to me. He's a really good off-spinner and he opens the batting. Cal's talking to Frankie, our non-stop joker and wicket-keeper. Frankie's sister, Jo, doesn't play in the team – she's our scorer and secretary and club organiser. Between Jo and Frankie is Ohbert, who comes from outer space where they don't play cricket.

We play at the Eastgate Priory Club and we should really be called Eastgate Priory Under 13s but Glory Gardens has been our name right from the very beginning. It comes from the Glory Gardens Rec at the back of my house, where most

Back Row: **Cal, Clive, Jacky, Erica, Mack, Tylan**
Front Row: **Frankie, Ohbert, Gatting, Jo, Hooker, Azzie,**
Matthew, Marty

of us started playing cricket.

There's one other important person I should tell you about who's not in the picture – our trainer, Kiddo Johnstone. Kiddo's the Priory's best batsman; he used to play county cricket and he coaches us at Nets every Saturday. In the week he turns into one of our school teachers. Frankie says that he's like Dr Jekyll and Mr Hyde and that it must be something he has for breakfast that mutates him into a teacher.

After Nets I found Kiddo in the club kitchen giving Gatting a bowl of water. Gatting's our most faithful fan. Well, maybe not a fan exactly but he comes along to all our games and to net practice, too. That's him in the picture, sitting in front of Ohbert. He's getting a bit ancient these days and he spends most of his time eating or snoring under the pavilion steps. But for some reason, given he's rather fat and smelly and sleeps most of the time, Gatting is everyone's favourite dog. He belongs to Kiddo and follows him everywhere.

Gatting was making such a racket, slurping water everywhere and pushing the bowl about with his nose, that Kiddo and I could hardly hear each other speak.

"I've got something to show you, kiddo," shouted Kiddo and, before I could say anything about fixtures, he handed me a letter. "Read that."

DURBANVILLE C.C.

Dear Prof,

I think I told you our under 13s are in England on tour for a month. Now I've just heard there's a problem with their itinerary. Can you fix them up with somewhere to stay for a couple of weeks – and maybe find them a few games of cricket? Sorry it's short notice, but if anyone can do it you can.

Please call.

Yours

Jim Winstanley

"It came this morning," said Kiddo. "What do you think?"

I jumped out of the way of Gatting's flying water bowl and read the letter again. "Who's Prof?" I asked.

"It's just a stupid nickname I had when I played cricket," said Kiddo.

"Why Prof?"

"Oh, I can't remember. Does it matter?"

"Not really. Where's Durbanville?"

"In South Africa. I used to coach there in the winter. What do you say? Could we find them all somewhere to stay?"

"You bet," I said. "When are they coming?"

"Next Saturday. There's not much time."

"And when can Glory Gardens play them?" I asked.

"The Wednesday evening, probably."

When Kiddo told the others there was an enormous cheer. Everyone wanted to have a Durbanville player to stay.

"We've got plenty of room," said Jacky. "My brother's away camping."

"We haven't got a spare bedroom," said Jo, "but Francis can move out and sleep in the bathroom."

"We could take two if you hang upside down in the broom cupboard," said Frankie.

I wouldn't fancy moving into Frankie's bedroom – it's a complete bombsite. Frankie is the most untidy, disorganised person I've ever known. He drives Jo mad because she's the exact opposite; she organises everything, including Glory Gardens C.C.

"How about you, Ohbert?" said Cal. "How many can you take?"

Ohbert was plugged into his Walkman as usual and concentrating hard on trying to read the writing on the bottom of his trainers. He looked up. "Oh but . . . what, Cal?"

"Do you want a South African to stay with you?" shouted Cal.

"A what?"

"A South African."

"Oh but . . . all right. But it won't eat my goldfish will it?"

Kiddo looked at Ohbert and frowned. "Well, er, before you get carried away, I think maybe your families might want a say in all this. Tell them about it when you get home and ask them all to ring me."

Moments later Mr Nazar, Azzie's dad, arrived, closely followed by Clive's aunt. They were the first two to sign up for the South Africans. Clive lives with his aunt these days. His mother died in a car crash years ago and he had a terrible time with his father after that. His old man used to get drunk and beat him up and in the end Clive ran away from home. He never talks about it and I think his father's probably left town now. Clive is a brilliant left-handed bat – although maybe not quite as brilliant as he thinks he is. He's a bit too keen to boast about his cricketing ability and criticise everyone else and his arrogance upsets some people in the team. There've been times when that's caused big trouble for us, but fortunately he's not as bad now as he used to be.

Anyway, everyone agrees that Clive's dead lucky to be living with his aunt; for a start, she makes the best cakes in the world. She said she'd take at least two South Africans and she'd got lots of friends who'd put more of them up if we wanted. Then she gave us Saturday morning's second bit of good news.

"If you really want to play against a good team you'd better take a look at this," she said putting on her glasses to read the Gazette.

WANT TO PLAY THE WEST INDIES?

Some of the boys from Griffiths Hall School, Barbados – who are in England for a special summer school – are missing their cricket. They are one of the top young sides in Barbados and they are offering to challenge any Under 13s team in the area.

"It gives a telephone number here," said Clive's aunt.

"South Africa *and* the West Indies," gasped Jo.

"It'll be just like the World Cup," said Frankie doing a little dance to celebrate.

"Outrageous," said Tylan.

"Too true it's outrageous," said Mack. "You can't have a World Cup without Australia."

Mack's family have been over here for a year now but he never lets us forget he's an Aussie. He goes to Clive's school on the other side of town and it was Clive who introduced him to Glory Gardens. He's the best fielder in the side and not a bad batsman and bowler.

"And what about India and Pakistan?" said Azzie's dad who's crazy about cricket and was getting very excited.

"Oh that's okay," said Frankie. "We'll just fly them in. Money's no problem. We've got plenty in the post office account, haven't we, Matt?"

Matthew's the club treasurer. "Thirty-eight pounds and 25p exactly," he said, putting on his serious, treasurer's face. "And we need a new cricket bat." Matthew opens the batting with Cal and he's just as serious when he does that.

"Oh well, maybe not," said Frankie. "I know! We'll ask Wyckham Wanderers to play and we can call them Australia and give them another thrashing."

"You know, that's not such a bad idea," said Mack.

"Really?" said Frankie, looking surprised.

"I know quite a lot of Australians over here. I might be able to put together an Aussie side."

"And I can pick a team to represent India and Pakistan," said Azzie's dad looking delighted at the idea.

"Well I'm not playing for them," said Azzie. "I play for Glory Gardens." That was a relief. Along with Clive, Azzie's our best batsman. We certainly couldn't afford to lose him as well as Mack.

"Hold on a minute," said Kiddo. "Before you all get carried away, we haven't got *any* teams coming yet. Let's wait and see what happens." He said he'd phone the West Indies school and talk to the fixtures secretary about arranging the games at the Priory.

But everyone was already making plans for the World Cup. Even gloomy old Marty was excited about it. "I wonder what the West Indian bowlers will be like? Fast, I bet," he said. Marty's our opening bowler and he's pretty quick himself.

As we walked home from Nets, Cal, Marty and I talked about nothing else. How good would the South Africans and West Indians be? Could Mack and Azzie's dad really get two more teams together? Would our parents agree to have a Durbanville player staying with us? Of course they would.

"By the way, did you know Kiddo used to be called Prof when he played cricket," I said.

"I bet it's because he teaches French," said Marty.

"Why?"

"Prof's short for *professeur* which means teacher," said Marty.

"But he only started teaching after he gave up cricket, didn't he?" I said.

"Just shows some people are born to be teachers," said Cal. "His mum probably called him Prof when he was little."

"Anyway, he doesn't like being called it much," I said.

"Oh really," said Cal. "I must tell Frankie."

Chapter Two

"Griffiths Hall School are definitely on, kiddoes," said Kiddo two days later. "I've sorted out the fixtures. We can play all the games at the Priory at a push – though I wouldn't mind using a second ground if we can find one."

Kiddo spread a big sheet of paper across his dining table.

GROUP A	GROUP B
Wednesday August 3rd	
Glory Gardens v Durbanville	
Thursday August 4th	
	Griffiths Hall v Team X
Friday August 5th	
Glory Gardens v T McCurdy's XI	Mr Nazar's XI v Griffiths Hall
Sunday August 7th	
T McCurdy's XI v Durbanville	Mr Nazar's XI v Team X

Wednesday August 10th

SEMI FINALS

Group A Winner v Group B Runner-up
Group B Winner v Group A Runner-up

Saturday August 13th
FINAL
All 20 over games except the final which will be 40 overs.

Kiddo had asked us to come to his house to talk about the 'World Cup' and Frankie, Cal, Erica, Azzie and I were gathered round looking at his plan.

It was the first time any of us had seen where he lived. It looked more like the Priory pavilion than a proper home. There were cricket pictures all over the walls – mostly photos of Kiddo when he was younger, playing county cricket. There he was receiving trophies or standing next to famous people like Geoffrey Boycott and Bob Willis. There was hardly any normal furniture in the room, just the big long table and three old battered leather armchairs. The carpet was worn out, too.

"Who are team X?" asked Erica.

"That's one of the things I wanted to talk to you about," said Kiddo. "Even if Asif's father and Mack come up trumps with their teams, we'll still need another side to make the whole thing work properly."

"I'm sure Wyckham Wanderers would play if we asked them," I suggested.

"Good idea," said Kiddo. We could play some of the games on their ground, too. That might bring a smile back to Bunter's face." Bunter Elgood is the Priory groundsman. He hates having too many games arranged on *his* ground; he says it wears out the square. I don't think he really likes people playing cricket at the Priory at all.

"What about the other two teams?" asked Kiddo.

"Dad says he's got his eleven already," said Azzie. "He's spent all week ringing people up from work. Mum says he'll get the sack if he's not careful. I think he's been having some secret training sessions with them, too."

"That wouldn't surprise me," said Kiddo with a smile. "How's young McCurdy getting on?"

"Last time I saw Mack he'd only got five," said Cal.

"I shouldn't worry – he'll find a team all right," said Erica.

"So it looks as if we've got a competition, kiddoes," said Kiddo.

"The World Cup!" insisted Frankie.

We all wanted to know about the West Indian team. Kiddo told us they would probably be the best team we'd ever played. "Everyone's good at cricket in Barbados," he said. "And they tell me Griffiths Hall School has one of the best teams on the island."

"Wait till they meet the best team in England," said Frankie.

"At least we won't be playing them until the semi-finals or maybe even the final," said Cal.

"If we get that far," said Erica.

"'Course we will," said Frankie. "We've only got to beat Mack's Aussies and the South Africans."

"I shouldn't underestimate Durbanville, kiddo," said Kiddo.

"When are they getting here?" I asked.

"On Saturday," said Kiddo. "I told them to join us at Nets, so you'll be able to get a good look at them then."

———— • ————

At Saturday Nets Mack announced he had nearly a full team. "It hasn't been easy, mind. There aren't as many Aussies over here as I thought. And most of them can't play cricket or else they're the wrong age."

"How many have you got?" asked Tylan.

"Nine. But a couple of them are only *just* Australians."

"How can you be only *just* Australian?" asked Erica.

"Well . . . if your grandmother's one, for instance."

"Or if you can sing *Waltzing Matilda* or you've got corks hanging down from your hat?" suggested Frankie.

"Well, I can't be too fussy if I'm going to find eleven players. I was thinking of picking Sam Keeping."

"He's not even a bit Australian, is he?" asked Cal.

"Not as far as I know," said Mack. "But he's the best wicket-keeper in the county and I've discovered his middle name's Sidney."

"So?"

"Well Sydney's in Australia, isn't it?"

"Have you got any real Australians apart from you?" asked Jo.

"Yes, loads. You wait and see. The Aussies are going to take this World Cup apart."

"Get ready to be blitzed by Glory Gardens on Friday," said Frankie. "First we get the Ashes back – then we win the World Cup."

Marty, Jacky and I spent most of the session working on our bowling action with Wingy, the first team's ace fast bowler.

"If you're going to bowl fast you've got to work at being aggressive," said Wingy. "That doesn't mean you have to swear at the batsman or anything like that. But remember, if you're a fast bowler, *you don't like batsmen*."

He told us to go and bowl as fast as we could and then he gave us a few individual tips. He told me to aim at the stumps by looking outside my right arm before I delivered the ball (I'm a left-arm bowler – even though I bat right-handed). And he showed Jacky how to follow through down the pitch.

Half way through Nets they arrived. The South Africans poured out of their minibus and rushed over to meet us. The first things I noticed were their stange accents and how fit they all looked. Their captain was about to introduce himself to me when a much shorter boy with thick, wavy hair and a biggish nose jumped in front of him. "This is Louis Moyake, captain of the invincible Durbanville Darts and I'm Joe Reddy, the best wicket-keeper in South Africa. You've probably heard lots about me already."

Louis gently pushed Joe out of the way. He was tall and athletic looking and he had teeth that were so white they

17

almost dazzled you when he smiled. Louis introduced the rest of his team and then I called out the names of the Glory Gardens players.

"Best wicket-keeper in England," shouted Frankie when I came to him.

"Heaven help England," muttered Cal.

The follow-through is very important to a fast bowler. Jacky lands on his left foot in the delivery stride and follows through on to his right. His hips swing round from right to left. Be careful not to run on to the pitch or to pull away too far to the off-side. Look how much Jacky's back bends and the shoulders swivel to give him maximum power.

There were too many of us to carry on with any serious training, but the South Africans quickly got changed and we batted and bowled in the Nets for an hour or more. I had a bat so that I could get a good look at their bowlers. They had several useful ones, especially a quickie named Johnny Malan who let out an ear-splitting grunt each time he released the ball. I noticed that all their batsmen liked to attack and get on the front foot to drive whenever they had the chance. Louis in particular looked like a class player. He uses his height and reach well when he bats and he's got powerful forearms and hits the ball every bit as hard as Clive does. I could see that even Clive was impressed – and that takes something special.

Nets came to an end when the cars started turning up. Kiddo had arranged for a big welcome for the South Africans and all our families came along to pick them up. Kiddo read out a long list of who was staying where. I got Louis Moyake which was only right because we were both captains. The two wicket-keepers were together, too – Frankie and Joe Reddy. They already seemed to be getting on well. Joe was showing Frankie and Tylan how to juggle with three cricket stumps. He nearly managed to skewer Gatting before Kiddo took the stumps away. There must be something about being a wicket-keeper that affects the brain. Most of them seem to be mad – but Joe turned out to be the craziest of them all.

It took ages to sort out all the luggage and get everyone in the right cars. Ohbert's dad, who looks like a tall, thin Ohbert with glasses, but without the baseball cap, started to drive off with a suitcase on the roof of his car. Then he backed into Clive's aunt's Metro which turned out to be a good choice because she just laughed and told him not to worry about the dent. "Thank you," choked Ohbert's dad, nodding at Clive's aunt out of the window of his car and rolling up the window at the same time.

"What's his name again?" I asked Louis, pointing to the pale-faced boy with fair, straight hair and a worried look who was sitting next to Ohbert in the back seat, his eyes growing wider and wider as he was driven off to Ohbert's house.

"Brad Miller, our opening bat. He's a bit shy."

"Poor devil, he'll never be the same again," said Cal, shaking his head.

"I'd rather live with the Addams family any day," said Tylan.

Johnny Malan, their big fast bowler was staying with Cal. The two of them came to our house for lunch with me and Louis. Fortunately, my sister was out. I showed Louis and Johnny the plans for the World Cup and we talked for hours about all the other teams in the competition.

"This is going to be the highlight of the tour," said Louis. "Who'd have thought we'd come to England and play against the West Indies, Australia and Pakistan and India."

"Not to mention Glory Gardens," said Cal.

Chapter Three

Wednesday was the day of our first World Cup match – against Durbanville. By then it seemed the South Africans had been staying with us for years.

I like them all but Louis is my favourite, so it's lucky he's staying with me. He's very generous and funny, too – in a quiet sort of way – and he's always smiling. If there is anything wrong with Louis it's that he's a bit too keen. For instance, he likes to get up at seven o'clock in the morning and go running with my Dad. Nothing would get me out of bed at that time of day in the holidays. I think they're both round the twist. He also knows more about cricket than anyone I've ever met – even Azzie's dad. On Sunday evening we had a Cricket Questions of Sport competition at the Priory. It was South Africa against England; Kiddo read out the questions. Durbanville won easily thanks to Louis. He could even answer questions like "Who scored the fastest triple hundred ever in a test match?", and "Which two players have scored a hundred and taken 10 wickets in a test?",

It isn't surprising he's so good because he spends his whole life reading *Wisden* when he's not playing cricket. The good thing is that it's driving my sister completely mad.

"Louis is even worse than you!" said Lizzie suddenly at breakfast. He'd just asked her "How many runs did Graeme Pollock score in his test career?", which isn't the sort of question Lizzie's good at.

"He's got a cricket book for a brain," she moaned.

21

"Cricket, cricket, cricket – that's all you two ever think about. You don't know a thing about anything else."

"Oh yeah, try me then," I said.

Lizzie thought for a moment. "Right . . . when was Julius Caesar born?" That's not fair, I thought, she's just been doing Roman history at school.

"Easy," said Louis. "102 BC." Lizzie's face fell. "It's the same as England's lowest score against India, see," said Louis. "102 in Bombay in 1981."

Lizzie put her head in her hands and I nearly fell off my chair laughing.

"Sorry, Lizzie," said Louis, "I sometimes forget you're not really interested in cricket." That's the understatement of the century. I sometimes pray that Lizzie will become more like Erica or Jo but it's hopeless. She's doomed to go through life hating cricket.

Although Louis is captain of Durbanville he's really quite shy – unlike Johnny Malan next door. You never have to ask where Johnny is, because you can always hear him. His voice comes straight through the wall from Cal's house. Cal says his dad is thinking of getting some ear plugs or moving out for the fortnight. Suddenly we heard him loud and clear. "I can't understand anyone who doesn't like cricket," he said. Louis and I looked at Lizzie and laughed.

———————— • ————————

At last it was time for the match. The Glory Gardens team picked itself. With Mack captaining the Australians we had only 11 to choose from and that included Ohbert. This is the team in batting order:

Matthew Rose	– steady opening bat
Cal Sebastien	– opening bat and off-spinner
Azzie Nazar	– stylish, high-scoring batsman
Clive da Costa	– left-hand bat, bowls a bit

Erica Davies	– all-rounder
Hooker (Harry) Knight	– captain and all-rounder
Frankie Allen	– wicket-keeper
Tylan Vellacott	– leg-spin bowler
Jacky Gunn	– fast bowler
Marty Lear	– fast bowler
Ohbert (Paul) Bennett	– hopeless

The game was supposed to start at 5pm but when we got to the ground, we found a photographer and a journalist from the Gazette waiting for us. A few minutes later the local radio reporter turned up, too. Someone must have told them about the World Cup – it might have been Matthew's mum because she works for the Gazette.

Louis and I had to do a radio interview which wasn't easy because Frankie and Joe kept butting in all the time. You couldn't really blame them for making a joke of it though, because the interviewer asked a load of really stupid questions.

"When you grow up, do you want to play cricket for England?" he said pointing his microphone at Louis.

"He's South African," I said.

"Makes no difference," said Joe. "All the best English players are South African."

"Who's your favourite player?" the reporter asked me.

"Ohbert Bennett," said Frankie.

"Oh, really? Who does he play for?"

Louis and I couldn't get a word in and eventually the reporter just gave up and started interviewing Frankie and Joe instead.

"Who's going to win the . . . your er . . . World Cup?" he asked.

"Morning, everyone," said Frankie, sliding into his Richie Benaud voice. "My word yes, there's no doubt about it, this is going to be a tough contest. I must say I wouldn't like to bet on the winner at this stage."

Louis and I went off to toss followed by the Gazette photographer. He made us spin the coin six times before he was happy that he'd got a good shot. Louis won the real toss and decided to bat.

When we got back to the pavilion, Frankie and Joe had completely taken over the interview. "Just about anything can happen in these limited over games," said Frankie 'Benaud'.

"Yes, my word. There's a lot of cricket between now and the Final. But they tell me the West Indies are the favourites," said Joe – his 'Richie Benaud' was even better than Frankie's.

"Glory Gardens look a strong team to me," said Frankie. "I particularly like the look of their young wicket-keeper, Frankie Allen. My, what a fine prospect he is. We'll be hearing more about him in this series, unless I'm much mistaken."

The reporter was looking increasingly desperate. I'm sure he'd never even heard of Richie Benaud or any other cricketers for that matter – so it was all a complete mystery to him. And when Joe started singing the South African national anthem, he finally gave up, packed up his equipment and left.

At least the journalist from the Gazette seemed to know something about the game. She spent ages talking to Kiddo and writing it all down in a little note book.

It was nearly six o'clock when the match finally got under way and Louis and Brad Miller walked out to bat. Brad was looking paler than ever. He had a sort of hunted look in his eyes and he seemed to have completely lost the power of speech. Ohbert followed him everywhere like a puppy; he very nearly went out to bat with him.

I'd have probably preferred to bat first because the Priory pitch looked full of runs and I like to get a score on the board and then put pressure on the other team. I set an attacking field for Marty's first over – with two slips and a gully – hoping to get an early wicket. Marty has been bowling fast and straight for the Colts and taking stacks of wickets. He got Louis to edge one to the slips early on but the ball dropped just short of Azzie and went for two runs.

Then Frankie put down a sitter off Jacky who came on from the Woodcock Lane end. It wasn't an expensive mistake though because Jacky immediately got one to nip back off the pitch; it just brushed Brad's pads, caught the inside edge of his bat and deflected onto the middle stump. Brad took a sad look at his shattered wicket and walked off. His heart must have sunk as he saw the figure of Ohbert coming towards him from the boundary. "Oh but, well batted, Brad," he said.

Johnny Malan came in to join Louis.

"Middle and leg," he boomed at the umpire. Johnny looks a big hitter and immediately he opened his shoulders and lifted Jacky over mid-wicket for four.

Marty had a good shout for lbw next over and Tylan dropped a difficult catch, low and hard at mid-on. But they still took eight off the over. Johnny Malan was just laying into everything and each time he called for a run we jumped as his voice echoed round the ground. Louis was quite happy to stay there and push the singles. With my attacking field there were plenty of gaps for him to run the ball into, so I dropped the slip and gully for Jacky and he bowled a tight line outside the

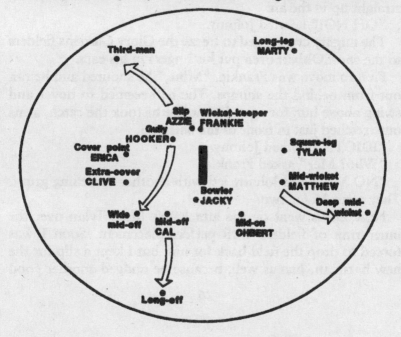

off-stump. We kept the run rate down a bit – but they still reached 20 at the end of the fourth over. I decided to vary the attack and give Tylan a bowl, leaving Marty with two overs for the end of the innings.

It's always a gamble bringing Tylan on because, like a lot of leg spinners, he usually bowls some rubbish mixed in with the good stuff. And he hadn't bowled in a match for over three weeks.

His first ball was a huge wide, miles down the leg side. But after that he found a good line and managed to turn the ball a bit. A swing from Johnny Malan just lobbed over Clive at square-leg and then Tylan went past Louis's outside edge twice in a row with two perfect leg breaks which bounced and turned.

Jacky was still bowling quite fast, skidding the ball through and hurrying both batsmen. The scoring rate slowed and the game got tenser. You could feel it. The ball wasn't getting past the field any more and we were cutting off the singles, too. Finally the pressure got to Johnny and he took a horrible swing at a good length ball from Tylan and top edged it straight up in the air.

"OH NO!" howled Johnny.

The mighty cry seemed to freeze the Glory Gardens fielders to the spot. Ohbert even put his fingers in his ears.

First to move was Frankie. "Mine," he shouted and he ran out from behind the stumps. The ball seemed to hover and swing above him for ages. But at last he took the catch, arms outstretched just in front of the batsman.

"IDIOT!" boomed Johnny.

"Who? Me?" asked Frankie.

"NO ME," and Johnny left with another deafening grunt. They were 26 for two.

Now Louis went on the attack. He lifted Tylan over the inner ring of fielders with perfect placement. Soon I was forced to drop the field back for him but I kept a slip for the new batsman. Just as well, because he nudged another good

26

leg break from Tylan straight into Azzie's hands.

Jacky had completed his four overs and I came on at the Woodcock Lane end to replace him. Louis immediately pinged me back over my head for four. He grinned as I stared down the wicket at him.

"What do you expect when you bowl slow half-volleys," said Frankie. I took a deep breath and forced myself to concentrate. The next ball beat Louis outside the off-stump and he looked up and said, "Well bowled." He didn't score another run off the over.

Tylan finished his spell – 4 overs, 13 runs, two wickets – he'd bowled so well that it was difficult to think who could follow him. I was still thinking about whether to bring on Cal or Erica as I ran in and bowled to Louis again. Smack. He caught another half-volley in the middle of the bat. But this time the trajectory was lower. Instead of flying miles over my head, the ball travelled like a rocket past my right shoulder. I shot out my hand and the catch stuck. I threw the ball in the air and shouted, "OWZTHAT!"

"Great catch," said Louis. I don't think he could believe it wasn't four runs.

The next man in was Joe. "I thought Frankie said you couldn't catch," he said, slapping me on the back as he passed.

"Frankie's the one that can't catch," said Jacky with a scowl.

"What about that skier?" said Frankie.

"You mean the one Johnny lobbed into your gloves?" said Joe. I could have caught that blindfolded with two arms tied behind my back."

"I must try that," said Frankie.

Joe Reddy is probably the most unorthodox batsman I've ever seen. He stands with his bat sticking straight up in the air and when the bowler runs in he goes for a little walk – either across his stumps or down the wicket or even backwards towards square-leg. It can be quite distracting for the bowler because it's difficult to know what line and length to bowl at him. Sometimes he'll take three steps down the wicket and play a forward defensive shot, or he'll suddenly walk across his stumps and leg glance a ball well outside the off-stump. But, if Joe's batting is strange, his running between the wickets is even weirder.

The third ball I bowled him was on middle stump but somehow he managed to step back and flick it to the left of Cal at backward point. "Wait," shouted Joe. At the same time he pretended to set off on a quick single and then he stopped dead in his tracks. The batsman at the other end started running. "Two runs," shouted Joe as Cal picked up the ball. His plan was probably to fool Cal into shying at the stumps and giving away overthrows but he succeeded only in fooling his own team-mate. Cal looked up and saw the non-striker was half way down the track and he hurled the ball to me. The batsman suddenly realised Joe wasn't going to run. He turned and slipped. I caught the ball over the stumps and flicked off the bails. He was run out by half the pitch.

"You idiot," said Joe, adding insult to injury. The poor boy was speechless; he just looked at Joe in disbelief, picked himself up and, with a shrug, walked off.

All through his innings Joe kept up a constant conversation with Frankie – offering advice on his wicket-keeping; telling him where he was going to hit the next ball; suggesting improvements in the fielding positions. From anyone else it would be infuriating, but Joe gets away with it, maybe because he's mad.

Erica came on at the other end and was immediately into her groove. She just bowls a straight line and waits for batsmen to make a mistake.

"What's your favourite shot?" said Joe to Frankie.

"Reverse sweep," said Frankie mischievously.

"Next ball," said Joe.

And he played an extravagant reverse sweep to a ball from Erica on his leg stump. The ball was too short for the shot; he got an edge off the shoulder of the bat and the ball lobbed over Frankie's head. Joe laughed as he ran the single.

In my next over I had him miscuing in the air but Jacky dropped an easy catch at mid-off – it went straight to him and just bounced out of his hands.

"Hard luck, Jacky," said Joe, walking over to console him. "Took your eyes off the ball though, didn't you? Next time remember to watch it all the way into your hands." Then he went back to the crease and smeared my next ball through the covers for two. "Now that's better," he said to himself as he ran towards me.

There were two more near run outs – both Joe's fault. The second one was a real case for the third umpire but old Sid, the Priory umpire, gave Joe the benefit of the doubt. "Whew, that must have been close," said Joe to Frankie.

"Close? If it had been me I'd have walked," said Frankie. Joe laughed.

Erica bowled the next ball. Joe was down the track to it and then back on his stumps. The ball flicked his pad, then his bat and went through to Frankie who took a good catch. "Owzthat!" the whole of Glory Gardens went up for the appeal. The umpire looked and shook his head. "Off the pad," he said.

"And the bat," said Joe with a grin. And he turned, tucked his bat under his arm and walked. Frankie slapped him on the back as he went. "Thanks, Joe," he said. We clapped him off.

Durbanville were 56 for six with five overs to go. I asked Cal to bowl at my end, even though I still had an over to go. He dropped the ball on the spot immediately and bowled a maiden.

Apart from Ohbert, who dropped a sitter at square-leg and fell over chasing a ball to the boundary, the fielding was very tight. With Erica and Cal bowling well and keeping down the runs I couldn't make up my mind whether to bring Marty back or not. In the end I did and he repaid me. He took a wicket with the first ball of his new spell and then another with the last ball of the over; both clean bowled.

Cal bowled the twentieth and last over, varying his pace so well that it was difficult for the new batsmen to get him away – only three runs came off it.

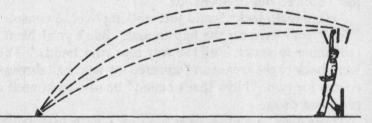

Cal varies his flight and pace cleverly to deceive the batsman. It's part of the armoury of all bowlers – especially spinners. If the bowler releases the ball early it will be projected upwards and present the batsman with the problem of where it will pitch and how fast it is travelling.

They finished on 73 for eight.

"Not enough on that track," said Louis to me as I led the team back into the pavilion. I wasn't too sure. It all depended on how well we played Johnny Malan and Co.

"Under four an over, kiddoes," said Kiddo coming into the changing room. "You know what to do."

"Score them in ten overs and have an early bath," said Frankie.

INNINGS OF DURBANVILLE........... TOSS WON BY VILLE WEATHER DULL

BATSMAN	RUNS SCORED	HOW OUT	BOWLER	SCORE
1 L. MOYAKE	2.1.1.·2.1.2.1.·2.2.1.·4.2.1	c & b	KNIGHT	23
2 B. MILLER	1.	bowled	GUNN	1
3 J. MALAN	4.2.1.2.1.1.1	ct ALLEN	VELLACOTT	12
4 B. DYANI		ct NAZAR	VELLACOTT	0
5 M. TANCRED	1	RUN	OUT	1
6 J. REDDY	2.1.3.1.1.2	ct ALLEN	DAVIES	10
7 A. McGLEW	1.1.1.2.1	bowled	LEAR	6
8 B. BRALENI	3.1.1	NOT	OUT	5
9 G. HENDRICKS	2	bowled	LEAR	2
10 P. VANDERMERWE		NOT	OUT	0
11				

FALL OF WICKETS											BYES	3·1·1·2	6	TOTAL EXTRAS	13
SCORE	6	16	35	43	45	56	66	70		10	LEGS	1·1·1	3	TOTAL FOR	75
BAT NO	2	3	4	1	5	6	7	9			WIDES	1·1	2	WKTS	8
											NO BALLS	1·1	2		

SCORE AT A GLANCE

BOWLER	SOWLING ANALYSIS ⊙ NO BALL + WIDE													OVS	MDS	RUNS	WKT
	1	2	3	4	5	6	7	8	9	10	11	12	13				
1 M. LEAR														3	0	13	2
2 J. GUNN														4	0	12	1
3 T. VELLACOTT														4	0	13	2
4 H. KNIGHT														3	0	12	1
5 E. DAVIES														3	0	8	1
6 C. SEBASTIEN														3	1	6	0
7																	
8																	
9																	

Chapter Four

Just as I expected, Johnny was fast. He was a good match bowler, too, with lots of the aggression that Wingy went on about. He bowled two short-pitched balls at Matthew and then yorked him with a beauty. It hit him on the toe of his boot and bounced off it on to the stumps.

At the other end Thomas Mhlongo came off six paces and bowled very nearly as quickly. He pitched the ball up more than Johnny and every delivery of his first over was on the stumps. It was all Cal could do to keep him out. Two maidens on the trot. But even at 0 for one I wasn't too worried. I knew the scoring would pick up if Azzie stayed at the crease.

He could easily have been out first ball. He went chasing a wide one outside the off-stump and edged it for four in the air just over slip's head. But soon Azzie started to time his shots and the faster Johnny and Thomas bowled at him the faster the ball came off his bat. A lovely cover drive scorched along the ground for three and then Azzie straight drove Johnny for two more.

Cal was defending carefully at the other end, taking quick singles to give Azzie the strike. Soon Louis was forced to go on the defensive against Azzie. He moved slip out to the cover boundary and dropped out a third man.

Mack arrived to watch the game just as Azzie leaned into another text book cover drive. "Nice one, Azz," he shouted.

"How many Aussies have you got, Mack," asked Tylan.

"The full eleven," said Mack. "And they can't wait to

demolish you lot on Friday."

"Are you giving them lessons in Australian?" asked
Frankie.

"No need, mate. They won't be doing a lot of talking – just
thrashing the Poms."

Johnny bowled a short one at Azzie and he pulled him for
four. The next ball was wide outside the off-stump and Azzie
went for a big cut. We heard the snick from the boundary. The
ball flew like a bullet high to Joe's right. He dived, took it
two-handed, rolled over and threw the ball up in the air. It
was a brilliant catch. And it stopped Azzie in full cry. He
nodded at Joe, put his bat under his arm and walked off.

Azzie goes after a wide, short-pitched ball and gets a top edge.
Joe Reddy takes this brilliant catch diving high to his right.
His eyes are following the ball as he takes it, baseball style.

33

We were 26 for two and Azzie had scored 19 of them.

Next over Cal got a horrible shooter and lost his middle stump. Suddenly the game had turned round completely. We had two fresh batters out there, Erica and Clive, and Durbanville really had their tails up.

Louis came on to bowl his little seamers and the run rate immediately dropped. It took Clive two whole overs to get off the mark. Clive's like Azzie, he likes to get on with it and he can easily get frustrated and play a stupid shot when he's bottled up like this. Mind you, to be fair to him, Erica was getting most of the strike.

"Come on, Clive," shouted Frankie from the boundary, "Wakey, wakey! No law against scoring runs, is there?" Clive glared at him, hands on hips and not amused.

There wasn't much either Clive or Erica could do anyway. The bowling was tight and the fielders extra keen; the ball seemed to be attracted to them as if it were on a string. Johnny Malan was amazing in the covers – he stopped one drive off the middle of the bat from Clive with a full length dive and managed to throw the ball in to stop the single, too.

"He's even better than Mack," said Tylan.

"Not possible," said Mack smiling.

Clive had one rush of blood and was dropped at mid-off but apart from that both he and Erica played sensibly, taking all the short singles they could and waiting for the bad ball which hardly ever came.

Clive is left-handed and Erica right which helped a bit; Louis had to keep changing his field after each run and the bowlers were forced to adjust their line. Luckily Erica and Clive are probably the quickest runners between the wicket in the team. They picked up some short singles which Matthew and Frankie, for instance, wouldn't have even attempted. But the run rate required still crept up – 4 . . . 5 . . . and now it was above 5 an over.

At last Clive got a bit of room outside the off-stump and he cracked the ball away though extra-cover for four. Even

Johnny couldn't beat it to the boundary, though he chased all the way and let out a great groan as his sliding save missed the ball by inches. Gatting, who was asleep at Kiddo's feet only yards away, leapt in the air with a howl and dived for cover under the pavilion. He hasn't moved so fast for years.

"Heavens, that boy's got a powerful voice," said Kiddo.

Erica played a delicate late cut for two and, with six overs left, we needed 26 runs to win. Louis tried a new bowler at the canal end and Clive immediately lifted him straight back over his head for three.

"If they can both stay there we'll win easily," said Cal.

"A pound says they will," said Frankie, who will gamble on anything from the number of cakes on the plate at tea to the colour of Ohbert's shorts.

"Oh, be quiet and watch the game, Francis," said Joe. She's the only person who can keep him even half under control. Frankie looked at her and rolled his eyes – but he did shut up.

In the next over Clive was dropped again – at square-leg this time by poor Brad Miller – playing a clipped forcing shot off his legs. It was quite an easy catch, too, and Brad was furious with himself. That seemed to jolt Clive into action. He almost went wild. First he pulled a ball off middle stump for four, then he drove savagely through mid-on for another boundary. 11 runs came off the over and suddenly we needed just 9 to win.

Erica pushed the first ball of the next over to backward square-leg's right hand and Clive, who was looking for the strike, called for a crazy single. It was suicide. Joe scampered up to the stumps and took the throw. Off came the bails with a quick flick of the wrist. Clive threw himself full length at the crease but he was way short of his ground. "OWZTHAT!" boomed Johnny from the boundary and Gatting barked from under the pavilion steps. The square-leg umpire raised his finger smartly. Clive got up and slapped his bat against his pad.

"I bet he says that he was in by a mile," said Frankie. And

judging by the look on Clive's face as he walked towards the pavilion, as usual *he* didn't think he was out.

I didn't have time to think about Clive, however, because I was in next. Nine to score off nearly four overs. It was no time for heroics.

"I'll try and give you the strike. You finish the job," I said to Erica.

She nodded.

I was nearly lbw first ball. I got only the thinnest edge of bat on the ball before it cannoned into my pads. Joe appealed from behind the stumps but luckily old Sid had heard the snick and shook his head. "Slice of luck there, skipper," said Joe.

I pushed the next ball into a gap on the leg side and got off the mark with an easy single.

Erica was seeing the ball beautifully now. Another finely played late cut brought her two more runs. She plays the shot brilliantly and bowlers hate it. It makes it very hard for them to contain the scoring by bowling just outside the off-stump.

The runs came slowly, but there was no hurry – neither of us was in any trouble and there were overs to spare. As the 19th over began I found myself facing, needing just three to win. The ball was pitched-up and I couldn't help myself. I launched into a straight lofted drive and hit it straight down long-on's throat. He took an easy catch. I'd scored just 2.

Frankie grinned at me as he passed on his way out to bat. "Just leave it to me, Hooker," he said.

A ball later he was walking back, too – caught on the mid-wicket boundary going for another death or glory shot. There was a delay while Tylan hurried to put his pads on. He'd assumed that he wouldn't need to bat. At last he set out to face the hat trick ball.

"Typical bad captaincy," said Frankie slumping back on his seat in front of the pavilion. "Putting me in to bat in the middle of a hat trick."

"It was a horrible shot," said Cal.

36

"I know," said Frankie, "but I wanted to hit a six in front of Joe."

"I can't see why. It wouldn't impress me," said Jo.

"I don't mean you, I mean Joe with an E," said Frankie. 'It's very confusing living with two people with the same name. I think you should move out."

"Oh thank you," said Jo. "Now be quiet. I want to concentrate."

Tylan saw off the hat trick with a nervous forward defensive and then ran like the wind for a leg-bye. A fine leg glance from Erica off the next ball saw us home. We'd won with an over to spare. Erica ended on 16 not out.

"Great game, Hooker," said Louis shaking hands with me. "But it would have been better if we'd held a few catches. You've got some fair batting, especially Azzie – what a cover drive!"

"Lucky they weren't relying on me," I said.

After we'd changed, Louis presented each of the Glory Gardens team with a baseball cap with Durbanville C.C. printed on the front. Ohbert was delighted with his. He got all the South Africans, starting with Brad, to sign it before he put it on, on top of the one he was already wearing. Louis also gave me a Durbanville pennant to hang in the pavilion and a tee-shirt which said 'Durbanville Tour of Britain' with a picture of an animal that Frankie called a reindeer but Louis said was an impala.

"Have you ever seen an impala, Brad?" asked Ohbert.

Brad looked at Ohbert with his two caps, his Walkman and his silly grin and just nodded silently. He'd scored one run, dropped a sitter and now he was going home with Ohbert.

INNINGS OF GLORY GARDENS   TOSS WON BY D'VILLE   WEATHER FINE

BATSMAN	RUNS SCORED	HOW OUT	BOWLER	SCORE
1 M. ROSE	»	bowled	MALAN	0
2 C. SEBASTIEN	1·1·1·2·1 »	bowled	MHLONGO	6
3 A. NAZAR	4·2·1·3·2·2·1·4 »	ct REDDY	MALAN	19
4 C. DA COSTA	1·1·2·1·4·3·2·4·4·2 »	RUN	OUT	24
5 E. DAVIES	1·1·1·1·2·1·1·1·2·1·2	NOT	OUT	16
6 H. KNIGHT	1·1 »	ct MHLONGO	BHALENI	2
7 F. ALLEN	»	ct VAN DE MERE	BHALENI	0
8 T. VELLACOTT		NOT	OUT	0
9				
10				
11				

FALL OF WICKETS

	1	2	3	4	5	6	7	8	9	10
SCORE	0	26	30	65	71	71				
BAT NO	1	3	2	4	6	7				

BYES	1·2		3	TOTAL EXTRAS	7
LEG BYES	1·1·1·1		4	TOTAL FOR	74
WIDES					
NO BALLS			WKTS		6

SCORE AT A GLANCE

BOWLING ANALYSIS ⊙ NO BALL + WIDE

BOWLER	1	2	3	4	5	6	7	8	9	10	11	12	13	OVS	MDS	RUNS	WKT
1 J. MALAN	W·	·4·	3··	·4·4	⊠									4	1	15	2
2 T. MHLONGO	W·	·1·	···	·2·	⊠									4	1	10	1
3 L. MOYAKE	1··	·1·	·4·	⊠										3	0	9	0
4 G. HENDRICKS	··1	1··	1·2·	·1·	⊠									4	0	19	0
5 M. TANCRED	3·1	1·2·												2	0	10	0
6 B. BHALENI	··1·	W·W												1·5	0	4	2
7																	
8																	
9																	

Chapter Five

"Right, let's see this famous Aussie team," said Cal to Mack. It was the next evening and the Durbanville and Glory Gardens players were all at the Wanderers ground watching the game between Wyckham Wanderers and the West Indians.

"You asked for it," said Mack. "Right hold your breath; this is Mack's Academy." He took a piece of paper from his pocket and showed us the list of names.

T. McCurdy (captain)	K. Hawkes
S. Keeping (wicket-keeper)	C. Bardsley
R. Mattis	R. Bardsley
K. Johansen	R. Carkeek
J. Darling	B. Woolf
W. Hyde	

"Sam Keeping, Rick Mattis *and* Bazza Woolf!" I gasped. We'd played against them all before. Rick's the captain of Old Courtiers and one of the best all-rounders in the League; Bazza and Sam both play for Mudlarks – though Sam's played for us a couple of times this year in the League. Bazza's a pretty quick bowler and Sam's the best keeper you'll ever see.

"Not one of them is Australian," protested Jacky.

"That's where you're wrong," said Mack. "Rick's grandfather lives in Melbourne – that qualifies all right."

"And Bazza?" asked Cal.

"Bazza would play for anyone," said Marty.

"Yeah, well I asked him if he wanted to play and he said yes. And when I told him he had to be an Australian, he said, 'That's okay with me, cobber.' So we sort of left it at that." Mack grinned and added. "It hasn't been easy getting a team together, you know. And most of them are proper Aussies."

"Who are these two?" asked Azzie, pointing at the two Bardsleys on the list. "Are they brothers?"

"No," said Mack, "but you're close."

"Sisters?" asked Erica.

Mack nodded. "Cheryl and Roz. And wait till you see them play."

"Brilliant," said Erica. "It'll be great not being the only girl on the field for a change."

"I've got another one," said Mack. "Kris Johansen. And she's even better than Roz and Cheryl. She bowls quicker than Marty for a start."

"Maybe," said Marty. "But I bet she's not quicker than *him*."

We all turned to watch Richard Wallace, the West Indian pace bowler who was storming up to the wicket. He was fast all right. So fast that, from where we were sitting, it was hard to pick up the ball from the moment it left his hand till the batsman played his shot.

Wyckham were struggling badly against Griffiths Hall School. They'd done pretty well to hold the West Indians to 103 off their 20 overs; that included a fifty from the Griffiths Hall captain, Victor Eddy. Just before he got out he looked as if he was going to take the Wyckham attack apart. But it was the bowling that was really devastating, especially the opening pair, Richard Wallace and Thompson Gale. Richard was like lightning. He wasn't tall but he ran in really fast and he had a beautifully smooth action with a lot of power in the shoulder. Apart from Liam Katz, none of the Wanderers had the first clue how to play him. The batting side had slumped to 21 for six off six overs; and Richard Wallace had already taken four of them. He'd just started his last over.

"I never thought I'd mind seeing Wyckham thrashed," said Frankie. "But the strange thing is, today I can't help feeling sorry for them."

"OWZTHAT!" There was another huge appeal for lbw and Richard Wallace got his fifth wicket. Win Reifer, Wyckham's quick bowler, walked out to bat.

"Knock him out of the ground, Win," shouted Frankie.

Win tried. He took a huge swing off the first ball and top-edged it over the keeper for four. He drove the next off a thick outside edge for another boundary. The third and last ball of the over was a very fast yorker. Win swung at it, missed and his middle and leg stump cartwheeled out of the ground. Win looked at the wicket, looked at the bowler, scratched his head and departed.

Louis had been watching the game quietly. He didn't seem too upset about last night's defeat, unlike Joe and Johnny who had been complaining about dropped catches and pathetic batting ever since.

"It's the worst we've played on tour," moaned Johnny.

"But it wasn't really a fair contest, was it?" said Frankie.

"What do you mean?" asked Johnny.

"12 against 10."

"What?"

"Didn't you know? Joe was playing for us." Frankie looked at Johnny with a completely straight face. "We slipped him a fiver to run everyone out."

"Oh but, I don't believe it!" said Ohbert. For once he'd been listening. "Wait till I tell Brad." We all laughed as Ohbert set off in pursuit of Brad who was sitting on his own.

Suddenly Louis said to me, "I think I know how to beat this lot."

"Who Wyckham?" I asked.

"No, the West Indians," he said. "They're good – but they're not unbeatable. You've got to look for the weaknesses."

"Such as?"

"Think I'm going to tell you?"

"Why not?"

"Because we're still in this competition. I just might tell you if you meet them in the final."

In the end Wyckham were all out for 40 – Wallace six for 16. Liam Katz was not out on 15 – he'd carried his bat right through the innings. He looked fairly sick as he passed us and, of course, Frankie couldn't resist winding him up. "Playing for your average were you, Katzy?" Liam scowled but it wasn't long before he was boasting about his innings and, as usual, telling everyone how wonderful he is.

"There's no problem playing bowling like that if you get yourself in line," he said.

"I thought I saw you jumping out of the way a few times," said Cal.

"Into the square-leg umpire's pocket," said Frankie.

"Like Katz on a hot tin roof," said Tylan.

"I was just bobbing and weaving," said Liam. "It's all down to technique, you see. And courage."

"My word," said Frankie, slipping into his Richie Benaud voice. "What a courageous effort that was. But in the end, it just wasn't good enough and Wyckham were completely destroyed by old-fashioned, raw pace."

Liam looked hard at Frankie. "Was it you, then?"

"Who?"

"The idiot on the radio this morning?"

"Don't tell me they broadcast that interview?" said Mack.

"Yes, at about 8 o'clock."

"No wonder I didn't hear it," said Frankie. "It's a bit early for me."

"What was it like, Liam?" asked Azzie.

"Awful . . . complete rubbish. I thought there was something wrong with my radio."

"You're a disgrace, Francis," said Jo.

"That's no way to talk to a radio star," said Frankie. "Did

you hear the bit where I said Wyckham Wanderers were the worst team I've ever played against?"

"No," said Liam.

"Pity, they must have cut it out."

We had a barbecue after the game. The Griffiths Hall team and Frankie ate most of it. Frankie's idea of a balanced diet is a hot dog in each hand but even he could hardly keep up with the West Indians.

"Don't they feed you where you're staying?" asked Cal watching Victor Eddy finishing off an enormous burger in three bites.

"Na," mumbled Victor. "E arlly geranifin tooyaor."

"Try English, we don't speak Barbadian," said Frankie.

Victor swallowed down a great mouthful. "I said, we hardly get anything to eat at all. And its Bajan."

"What is?"

"We say Bajan, not Barbadian."

"If you play like that when you're starving, what are you like on full stomachs?" asked Marty.

"Terrifying," said Thompson Gale with a laugh.

"I know," said Frankie suddenly, "we'll have a World Eating Cup, too. Each team chooses their contender and the world champion is the one who eats the most sausages."

"You're sick, Francis," said Jo, shaking her head sadly.

But Joe Reddy thought it was a great idea. "I'll eat for South Africa," he said.

Thompson Gale said he'd be the Bajan champion. "Anything for a good meal," he said with a laugh.

"Forget it," said Mack. "None of you stands a chance against Kipper Hawkes."

"Who's Kipper Hawkes?"

"The All-Australian junior kipper-eating champion," said Mack. "He'll gulp down more sausages than the lot of you put together."

"Is he in your side?" asked Jacky.

"Yes, he's our off-spinner." Mack smiled. "And he's so

wide he sometimes doubles as a sight screen."

Frankie declared that the Sausage Eating World Championship would take place after the South Africa v Australia game on Sunday. "I'm going into training straight away," he said, reaching out for another hot dog.

Chapter Six

On Friday, we played Australia – or Mack's Academy to give them their proper name.

They were a strange mixture. We all knew what to expect from Bazza, Sam, Rick Mattis and, of course, Mack himself, but the other seven were a complete mystery to us. The two tall blonde girls were obviously the Bardsley twins – they were identical. Even Mack couldn't tell them apart which was a bit of a problem for him – especially when it came to placing his field. But the two players who stood out most were Rex Carkeek and Kipper Hawkes. Kipper's so fat he's almost round and Rex is as thin as a twig and he must be six feet tall. They couldn't have looked less alike and yet they were the closest of friends.

Mack lost the toss and I put them in. He seemed quite pleased. "It's my first time as captain," he explained. "I wouldn't know what to do if I won." He scratched his head and looked at the pitch again. "You know I think I'll open the batting for a change. You never give me the chance."

The start of their innings was sensational. The track had a bit of extra bounce in it and Marty gave it everything. His third ball pitched just outside off-stump and swung and lifted enough for Mack to get a touch. The ball flew high and fast between Frankie and Azzie at first slip. They both dived for it. Frankie was just in front of Azzie and he got his right glove to the ball and knocked it up. Azzie changed direction almost in mid-air, thrust out his right hand and caught it as he rolled over on to his back.

"Hard luck, Mack," said Cal.

"Bet they couldn't do that again if they tried," said Mack, walking off with his bat over his shoulder. So much for his career as an opening bat, I thought.

Marty's next ball was a perfect yorker which knocked out the new batsman's middle stump, but before we could celebrate there was a loud shout of "No ball" and we saw old Sid Burns raising his arm to the scorer. Marty had overstepped.

Marty slowly measured out his run up again, grumbling to himself and scowling at Sid as he did it. The batsman was Rick Mattis and he can score fifties. Marty bowled another fast delivery and Rick played forward; it bounced off his front pad. "Owzthat!" Marty swung round with both fingers raised at Sid. "Not out" said the umpire. "Too far forward and probably down the leg side." Old Sid hardly ever gives an lbw when the batsman's on the front foot. Marty was white with rage and he grabbed his sweater from Sid and stormed off to his fielding position at long-leg.

Jacky bowled tightly and accurately at the other end. He was skidding the ball off the pitch and more than once he genuinely beat the bat for pace. His sixth ball was a little wider and Mack's opening partner hung out his bat and lobbed up an easy catch to Erica at point.

Then the luck seemed to desert us. Marty and Jacky continued to bowl beautifully. Marty was flat out – and that was half the trouble. The ball kept hitting the edge of the bat and flying wide of the fielders. A wild swing from Rick Mattis shot over Frankie's head for four; another just beat Azzie's despairing dive.

At the other end Cheryl Bardsley (Frankie asked her which one she was when she came in to bat) hit Jacky crisply off her legs for two and then Tylan missed a difficult diving catch at square-leg. To make things worse Marty kept overstepping the bowling crease, straining for extra pace. He gave away at least five no balls. Eventually I was forced on the defensive and, of course, immediately they started picking up loads of singles.

After eight overs Mack's Acks had 40 for two. Marty and Jacky had both bowled well but things were just not going our way. I had to do something to slow down the scoring.

I came on myself at the Woodcock Lane end and Cal took over from Jacky at the canal end. I set an even more defensive field but still they hit the ball off the edge, in the air, over the keeper – and got away with it every time. Fifty came up, then sixty.

"They'll score 150 if we don't do something," I said to Cal at the end of my third over.

"Bring on Ty. He did the trick in the last game," suggested Cal.

I couldn't think of anything better. "I'll try him at your end and switch you."

"Okay, but tell him to bowl straight."

One of Kiddo's boring sayings is 'cricket's a funny game'. At 62 for two with seven overs to go, this game didn't look a bit funny. Yet an over later we were back in it with a vengeance.

On his day, Tylan's one of the best bowlers in the side although, like a lot of leg spinners, he often bowls a couple of bad balls an over and so he can be expensive. But the good thing about Ty is that he always spins the ball hard and once he gets on top he's very dangerous.

His first ball swung gently into Rick Mattis and bounced – just enough to brush the batter's glove on the way through to Frankie. Frankie juggled with it, knocked it up and caught it with a cry of victory. He was still talking about his brilliant catch when Sam Keeping arrived at the wicket.

"Did you see that, Sam? Lightning reactions."

Sam laughed, "Have you ever caught an easy one in your life?"

"I think it's a miracle if he catches one at all," said Cal.

47

The wrist spinner needs to spin the ball hard. Start the action with the back of the hand facing the sky. As you spin the ball the back of your hand turns towards your face. Tylan bowls side on to the batsman and notice how he takes aim over his left shoulder.

"Even Jo's lost count of all the ones he's dropped."

Sam swung the second ball he received for four over square-leg and then, stepping back on his stumps, he tried another leg side heave. The ball straightened and hit him just under the knee roll of his back pad, plumb in front. Up went the umpire's finger almost before we could appeal.

That brought Roz, the other Bardsley twin, to the wicket. Her sister was still there on 15. Tylan bowled the fifth ball of his brilliant over. It turned past the edge of a groping forward defensive. The next ball was a bit wider and it was driven on the up sweetly past Clive in the covers. He turned quickly and gave chase but the shot was worth an easy two runs. Cheryl turned for the second and slipped. Roz was already on her way. "No," shouted Cheryl but then she scrambled to her feet and started running. Panic set in and suddenly they were both running in the same direction. Roz stopped. Cheryl turned again and just got her bat in as Clive's throw came in to Frankie.

"Bowler!" shouted Tylan. Frankie whipped off his glove and threw to Ty who demolished the stump with a great sweep of his arm. Roz was still stranded in the middle. She stared at her sister. "What a dumb idiot," she said.

"It wasn't my fault I slipped," said Cheryl.

They glared at each other for a while and then Roz slowly walked off with Cheryl scowling at her, her hands on her hips.

"Which one's out?" whispered Frankie to Cal.

"I don't know," said Cal. "And I'm not asking her. I thought identical twins were supposed to be best friends."

Cal came back at the top end and bowled a maiden. Ty went for only three off the next as the crazy flow of runs slackened. In his final over, Cal tempted the new batsman down the track with a high, floating delivery which he missed completely and Frankie took off the bails with a flourish. Four wickets had gone down for just 8 runs. That brought Kipper Hawkes to the crease.

Kipper doesn't look much like a cricketer. As well as being seriously round he also wears extra thick glasses. His first shot was a wild swing which made me think he couldn't see the ball at all. But then he played a perfect sweep shot all along the ground for four.

With three overs left I decided to stay with Tylan and bring Erica on for an over at the other end.

Four came off Tylan's third over. Erica had Kipper dropped by Matthew at wide mid-on. Then Kipper hoisted an enormous swing in the direction of deep mid-wicket. He and Cheryl had almost run two runs while the ball was still in the air. Under it, way out on the mid-wicket boundary was the lonely figure of Ohbert. Why had I put him there? He was running round in a circle looking up and shouting, "Oh oh oh." Finally he gave up and put his hands over his head and shut his eyes. The ball plummetted to earth missing him by inches. Ohbert didn't move.

"Throw it, you turkey," shouted Clive. Ohbert opened his eyes and picked up the ball. "Oh but, I missed it," he said. His feeble throw just reached Clive at square-leg who threw in so hard to Frankie that the ball went for an overthrow. Erica looked furious. She stared angrily at Clive but didn't say a word.

Tylan's last over started badly with a four driven straight back over his head. Deep mid-off was too wide to stop the boundary. Then Tylan beat Kipper twice in succession, turning the ball just past the outside edge of his bat. The fourth ball of the over went straight on. Kipper played for the turn and lost his off-bail. Two more runs came from the over and Mack's Acks finished on 90 for seven. Only three of them had scored double figures: Rick Mattis, Kipper and Cheryl Bardsley who was unbeaten on 23.

You'd think she'd got a golden duck from the way her sister greeted her at the end of the innings. If Frankie had been holding a World Cup swearing competition the final would have been between Roz and Cheryl.

"Don't worry," said Mack, "they're always like this. You wait until they really get mad."

"I'll take your word for it," said Cal.

INNINGS OF MACK'S ACADEMY   TOSS WON BY GG   WEATHER SUNNY.

BATSMAN	RUNS SCORED	HOW OUT	BOWLER	SCORE
1 T. McCURDY	»	ct NAZAR	LEAR	0
2 J. DARLING	2 »	ct DAVIES	GUNN	2
3 R. MATTIS	1·1·1·4·2·1·1·1·1·2·1·2·4·1·2· 1·(27) »	ct ALLEN	VELLACOTT	27
4 C. BARDSLEY	1·2·1·1·1·1·2·2·1·1·1·1·2·1·2·2·1	NOT	OUT	23
5 S. KEEPING	4 »	lbw	VELLACOTT	4
6 R. BARDSLEY	»	RUN	OUT	0
7 W. HYDE	»	st ALLEN	SEBASTIEN	0
8 J. HAWKES	4·3·1·4 »	bowled	VELLACOTT	12
9 K. JOHANSEN	1	NOT	OUT	1
10				
11				

FALL OF WICKETS

	1	2	3	4	5	6	7	8	9	10
SCORE	0	5	62	66	66	70	88			
BAT NO	1	2	3	5	6	7	8			

BYES	2·2·0·0·2·7	10	TOTAL EXTRAS	21
LEG BYES	1·1·1·2	5	TOTAL FOR	90
WIDES	1·	1		
NO BALLS	1·1·1·1	5	WKTS	7

SCORE AT A GLANCE

BOWLING ANALYSIS ⓒ NO BALL + WIDE

BOWLER	1	2	3	4	5	6	7	8	9	10	11	12	13	OVS	MDS	RUNS	WKT
1 M. LEAR				⊠										4	0	19	1
2 J. GUNN				⊠										4	0	13	1
3 H. KNIGHT				⊠										3	0	9	0
4 C. SEBASTIEN			⊠	M	⊠									4	1	13	1
5 T. VELLACOTT														4	0	17	3
6 E. DAVIES														1	0	4	0
7																	
8																	
9																	

Chapter Seven

Mack has one of the biggest families I know – five brothers and three sisters. And, except for his oldest brother, the whole family had come along to support Mack's Acks against Glory Gardens. They've also got three dogs and a parrot and they were all here, too. That made 14 of them in total including Mack. Mack said they'd brought the parrot because if they left it at home on its own it would sulk for weeks; it's very keen on cricket and always watches the test matches on the telly.

The parrot could say 'G'day' in an Australian accent and 'How awfully kind of you' in a posh English voice. But mostly it just squawked loudly and, now and then, it said something which sounded like 'Have the Poms for breakfast, mate.' Mack's mum looked embarrassed when it said that but it made his little sister laugh every time. The parrot sat on her shoulder all through the game.

Gatting hated the bird. He gave it one sniff and it tried to bite his nose. After that he kept well away but he growled and bared his teeth each time it spoke or squawked. He got on all right with the three dogs though. They were all black like him but about half his size and they bounced round him yapping as if they thought they were his own puppies.

"Now we'll see how good she really is," said Marty. Kris Johansen was about to open the bowling against Matthew. Her first ball was short and it whistled past his chest as he swayed out of the way of it.

"Phew! Mack's right, she's as quick as you," said Cal to Marty.

"But not such a lovely mover," said Frankie.

"How awfully kind of you," said the parrot, and we all laughed.

Matthew played out the over but he had to hurry his shots a couple of times and he took one on the thigh which must have made him glad he was wearing a thigh pad.

Rex Carkeek bowled from the other end. He's a left-armer and he bowls around the wicket with an awkward slinging action. He wasn't as fast as Kris but his height made it difficult for Cal and Matthew to judge the length and bounce.

"The trouble is he's so thin you can't see him running in to bowl," said Tylan.

We were all watching the bowling very closely. We knew it wasn't going to be easy. Even Azzie who's usually so calm before an innings was fiddling nervously with his gloves. Tylan was biting his finger nails and Clive paced up and down like a caged bear. Only Ohbert who was listening to his so-called personal stereo ignored what was going on on the pitch.

"Turn that thing down, Ohbert. It's making my ears buzz," said Jacky. But Ohbert didn't hear him.

Cal cut the last ball of the second over wide of Mack at cover point and called for a quick single. Matthew hesitated. "Wait," he cried. "Yes," insisted Cal. Matthew ran. If he'd gone straight away he'd probably have made it but Mack's throw came in right over the bails and the keeper beat Matt by a good yard. Matthew stared at Cal and said something under his breath before he returned to the pavilion.

Azzie hit his first ball right off the middle but straight to Mack – now at square-leg for the new over. Without a call Azzie ran. Cal was backing up well and was through for the quick single like a flash. But Azzie, with the fielder behind him, didn't spot the danger. Mack saw his chance and hurled a flat, left-handed throw at the bowler's wicket. It hit middle stump. Azzie couldn't believe his eyes but he was well out of his ground.

The Acks were delirious. They all rushed up and surrounded Mack. Cal stood alone in the middle, reflecting on the two run-outs. You couldn't say either of them had been his fault, especially the second, but there's nothing worse than a run-out to demoralise a team. I couldn't believe it. We all know Mack's an ace fielder – so why take chances like that with him. It was crazy.

Clive walked out with his usual swagger. We badly needed someone to get on top of the bowling and an innings from Clive with Cal holding up the other end would be the perfect answer.

Clive looked in good nick. He clipped the opening bowler off his legs for two and then pulled her through mid-wicket for three. He was just beginning to look set for a big innings when he drove rather loosely and on the up into the covers. The ball only just carried to Mack and he took a sharp, one-handed catch down by his right boot. He threw the ball up in delight. He had every right to be pleased – he'd now had a hand in every wicket so far, and we were 11 for three – the worst possible start.

Erica joined Cal and they battled away for two overs. But then Erica got one of those balls that can take anyone's wicket. It came in Kris Johansen's final over. Pitched on middle stump, it cut away just enough to flick the off-bail. "Good ball," said Erica but she prodded the pitch as she left, as if to say, it must have hit a bump.

20 for four – if ever we needed a captain's innings at number six, it was now. I took guard and looked round the field. Mack had left me some tempting gaps on the off-side. No doubt he was inviting me to nick one to the keeper or the slip.

I played forward to Kris's last delivery of her four overs. She got a round of applause from the Acks for her figures: one for 9 off four overs.

"Looks like one of us has got to score fifty," said Cal as we both went 'gardening' in the middle.

"I bet he'll bring Bazza on next over," I said. Bazza is a very useful bowler, quick and pretty accurate.

"Well, we're not going to win unless we get some runs on the board. I say we go for Bazza. Try and knock him off his length."

"Okay."

"Death or glory," said Cal.

The tall left-armer finished his tidy spell and, sure enough, Mack introduced Bazza from the Woodcock Lane end. His first ball was a loosener and Cal swung it away for four. A single brought me on strike and I drove Bazza twice through the covers.

Mack turned to spin at the other end and he measured out a more defensive field for Kipper Hawkes. Cal was on strike so I watched Kipper bowl. He was left-handed and he bowled round the wicket, running in between the umpire and the stumps. The umpire had to stand a long way back to let him through. As Kipper released the ball he made a noise, somewhere between a grunt and a squeak. His first ball was a full toss and Cal glanced it for a single. I took a new guard and watched carefully as Kipper ran in again. I reached forward for the ball, but I wasn't to the pitch and it looped off the edge for an easy chance to second slip, if there'd been one. Okay, I thought, so he can spin it. The next delivery was given a lot of air but I wasn't tempted and I played it defensively. Then a quicker one. Again I pushed forward to the pitch. But I knew we needed runs and we had to score them off the spinner as well as off Bazza. The last ball of the over gave me just a fraction of room outside off-stump and I flashed at it. I got a thick edge and it flew quickly to point. The fielder dived forward and took a great catch. I was out for four – two more than I'd got against Durbanville.

"Don't worry, Hook, we can still do it," said Cal.

"You mean *you* can do it," I said. I couldn't see anyone else scoring the runs.

Cal continued to go after Bazza and Frankie, who'd joined him, tried to do the same. Frankie had a slice of luck when he hoisted one in the air to Cheryl Bardsley at square-leg. As the ball was dropping Mack shouted, "Roz". Cheryl stopped at the last moment and the ball fell to the ground.

"Sorry, I meant Cheryl," said Mack. Cheryl was furious – but she didn't know whether to blame Mack or her sister.

As I feared, Frankie didn't have much of a clue against the spinner. He hoicked one over mid-off and then he was clean bowled going for a big heave across the line. Tylan lasted two balls and then was bowled playing outside a straight one.

"We're being Kippered," said Frankie as Jacky made his way to the wicket.

"Give the strike to Cal," Azzie shouted to Jacky.

Although Bazza was proving expensive, Mack kept him on. Why not? After all, he had plenty of runs to play with. I worked out that we needed 50 off eight overs – more than 6 an over and only three wickets left.

Jacky put up some resistance and the 50 came up in the fourteenth over. Cal was calling the shortest of singles which was risky because the Acks were very lively in the field, especially Kris Johansen and Mack in the covers. In the end, the Glory Gardens pair played their luck once too often; Jacky pushed a ball to Bazza's right and ran. Bazza picked up and threw down the stumps at his end for the third run out of the innings. Next ball Bazza knocked out Marty's off-stump.

So that was it. Ohbert hadn't even got his pads on. Tylan helped him but then he forgot his batting gloves and had to come back for them. He'd probably forgotten his box, too but no one could be bothered to remind him. Finally he trotted out to face the Australians. It was just a question of time before Ohbert got out. Frankie took bets that he would be bowled off the first ball he received.

Meanwhile Cal had the strike ... and strike he did. He went down the wicket to Kipper and hit him twice over the top.

*Cal goes for the big hit over the top. But he doesn't just swing
wildly at the ball. He keeps his eye on it all the time and hits
straight through the line. Look how his front foot is pointing
towards extra-cover. Even after the follow through he still has
his eyes on the ball.*

If Cal could knock a few we might at least lose respectably.
He was looking very determined and taking every run he
could – even with the handicap of Ohbert at the other end. He
was very nearly run out going for a quick single off Kipper. If
the throw had come in at the other end Ohbert would have
been out without facing a ball.

Then Kipper bowled to Ohbert. Ohbert played his text

book forward defensive with his nose only inches from the ground. As always, he played it to completely the wrong ball but Sam, the keeper, was so surprised he let it through for two byes. Frankie groaned and paid Azzie the 20p he owed him for the bet.

Cal had a long talk to Ohbert at the end of the over. Why he bothered no-one could imagine. We all know there's a dark tunnel between Ohbert's ears which doesn't connect to anything. Ohbert walked back to his crease, looked up at us and waved his bat.

"G'day," squawked the parrot.

"Someone put him out of his misery," said Clive.

"Who? Ohbert or the parrot?" asked Frankie.

Mack was forced to make two bowling changes. He went for Roz Bardsley at the top end.

"She can't bowl," said Cheryl to Mack. "You sure you don't mean me?"

Roz pulled a face at her.

Cal hit the first ball for four past point. "Told you," muttered Cheryl.

But it turned out that Roz wasn't a bad bowler at all. Cal had two swings and missed completely. Then he glanced the fourth ball fine and they ran three. That left Ohbert with two to face. He missed the first by a mile and it bounced over his leg stump. The next was quicker and straight and Ohbert swung with his eyes closed. I had my eyes shut, too, and when I opened them the ball was looping just out of the keeper's reach. They ran two more.

Now Cal was on 40 and we were 74 for nine and the impossible was, well, still impossible. But who knows, if Cal could hit another couple of boundaries and keep Ohbert from the strike. . . We needed 17 off three overs and suddenly it was so tense that we hardly dared breathe – we were on the edge of our seats.

Mack bowled from the canal end. He'd dropped his field right out to give the single that would put Ohbert on strike.

There were easy runs off the first three balls but Cal refused them all. Then he edged down to third-man. He ran the first fast but there was only one in it. Again Ohbert had two balls to face. In came the field. Mack bowled a slow looping delivery. The idea was probably to tempt Ohbert down the pitch and have him stumped by Sam. But any plan you make for Ohbert is likely to end in failure. Ohbert watched the ball in the air, stepped forward, then back and swung at it as it bounced. Astonishingly, he connected cleanly and it flew over square-leg for two. There was a huge cheer from the Glory Gardens supporters and Gatting barked loudly. He seemed very keen to drown out the parrot.

There was a big appeal for lbw off the last ball but this time Ohbert had gone for a walk down the wicket and he was well out of his crease. At the end of the over he went down the track to talk to Cal.

"He's giving Cal instructions now," said Jacky.

"I hope he's telling him to keep the strike," I said.

"That's it, Ohbert, tell him to pull his finger out," shouted Frankie. Ohbert waved again.

"G'day," said the parrot.

We needed 14 to win off 12 balls. Cal was still trying to hit twos and fours to keep the strike. He got a two running the ball down to backward square-leg. Then he missed a wide delivery down the leg side. For once Sam fumbled it but there was no need to run because the umpire signalled the wide. That didn't matter to Ohbert, of course. He was off, dashing down the wicket towards Cal. Cal hadn't seen him. He was watching Sam retrieving the ball.

"Cal run! RUN!" screamed Frankie.

Cal turned, saw the danger and galloped up to the other end. He just beat Sam's throw. Now Ohbert had three to face. He missed the first which, judging from the groans of the Acks, must have grazed his off-stump. Then he survived a huge shout for lbw. The last ball of the over was short and Ohbert sort of punched it with his gloves wide of Sam's despairing dive. Again he ran. "No" screamed Cal, who realised it was the end of the over and Ohbert would keep the strike. But it was no good, Cal had to run or throw away his wicket.

10 to win off the last over and Ohbert on strike. It had been fun while it lasted. But Ohbert wasn't finished. Somehow he managed to kick away Mack's first ball for a single whilst playing a shot several feet away from the ball. Cal pushed the next slowly down to deep square-leg and they got two as the fielder ran in from the rope. The third ball was blasted straight over the bowler's head. It looked a certain four but long-on ran round and cut if off with a slide just inside the boundary. Cal grabbed a third run on the throw which was probably a mistake, but at this stage every run mattered.

4 to win and once again Ohbert was facing. This time Mack tried a quicker delivery. Ohbert played his forward defensive and the ball hit his glove. It hung in the air for an awfully long time and Sam leapt forward for the catch but Ohbert fell over in front of him and blocked his way. Two balls left. Again the batsmen met in the middle. Whatever happened they had to run this time.

Cal started running as the ball was bowled. Ohbert jumped down the pitch as if he was setting off on a run, too. He met it on the full and it cannoned off a whirl of pad and bat to short mid-off. Cal was through like lightning and he ran his bat in just before the ball hit the stumps.

Frankie was going out of his mind. "Three to win! Three to win! Swing it this way, big man," he shouted to Cal. Everyone was on their feet. The parrot cried "G'day", Gatting barked, the McCurdy dogs ran round in circles.

Mack took ages to move his field out to the boundary. At last he ran in and bowled. Cal went down the track and connected. The ball rose high in the air. Was it a six? No it was going to drop short. The fielder on the mid-wicket boundary stood waiting.

"It's Roz," said Azzie.

"Or Cheryl," said Frankie.

Roz or Cheryl misjudged the length. She was too far back; she was going to miss it. At the last moment she lurched forward and caught the ball on her knees, but she caught it cleanly. Cal stopped running. Ohbert carried on. Glory Gardens groaned. Mack's supporters cheered. The parrot said, "Have the Poms for breakfast, mate."

Ohbert was still running but everyone else was walking off. Cal shook hands with Mack. The batsmen had nearly completed two runs when the catch was held but, of course, they didn't count. We finished on 88 – just two runs short. And Cal had scored 48. It had been one of the great innings – the best I'd ever seen him play.

HOME TEAM	GLORY GARDENS V MACK'S ACADEMY	AWAY TEAM	AT FASTGATE 7000 DATE AUGUST 5TH

INNINGS OF ...GLORY GARDENS...   TOSS WON BY ..G.G.... WEATHER ..SUNNY

BATSMAN	RUNS SCORED	HOW OUT	BOWLER	SCORE
1 M. ROSE	1·	RUN	OUT	1
2 C. SEBASTIEN	1·1·1·1·1·4·1·2·1·1·3·2·1·1· 1·2·4·4·1·(55)·4·3·1·2·2·3	ct R. BARDSLEY	McCURDY	48
3 A. NAZAR		RUN	OUT	0
4 C. DACOSTA	2·3·1·2	ct McCURDY	CARKEEK	8
5 E. DAVIES	2·2	bowled	JOHANSEN	4
6 H. KNIGHT	2·2	ct HYDE	HAWKES	4
7 F. DAVIES	2·1·2	bowled	HAWKES	5
8 T. VELLACOTT		bowled	HAWKES	0
9 J. GUNN	1·1	RUN	OUT	2
10 M. LEAR		bowled	WOOLF	0
11 P. BENNETT	2·2·1·1	NOT	OUT	6

FALL OF WICKETS												BYES	·1·2·		4	TOTAL EXTRAS	10
SCORE	2	2	11	20	53	41	41	54	54	89		LEG BYES	·1·1·1·		4	TOTAL FOR	88
BAT NO	1	3	4	5	6	7	8	9	10	2		WIDES ·1· / NO BALLS			2	WKTS	10

SCORE AT A GLANCE

BOWLER	1	2	3	4	5	6	7	8	9	10	11	12	13	OVS	MDS	RUNS	WKT
1 K. JOHANSEN														4	1	9	1
2 R. CARKEEK														4	0	10	1
3 B. WOOLF														4	0	24	1
4 J. HAWKES														4	0	15	3
5 R. BARDSLEY														2	0	13	0
6 T. McCURDY														2	0	9	1
7																	
8																	
9																	

Chapter Eight

It all started when Frankie bought a Mars bar on the way to Nets on Saturday morning. Joe was fooling about and he grabbed it and somehow it got thrown in the road and a car ran over it and flattened it. It's not even a busy road and it was just bad luck that the car was passing at that precise moment. But of course Joe laughed his head off. He peeled the squashed Mars bar off the road and held it up in front of Frankie's nose.

"You'll be sorry you did that," said Frankie. He wasn't really angry but if there's one thing Frankie cares about in the world it's his food. Joe licked his lips and took a big bite of the extra long, thin Mars bar.

"Mmmmm, lovely."

"From now on, Joe Reddy, just remember one thing," said Frankie. "Wherever you go your life's in danger."

Joe held up his hands, a look of pretend horror on his face.

"This is war," said Frankie. "I mean it."

"To the death!" said Joe. And they shook hands. I wasn't sure what they meant but I had a feeling that Frankie's and Joe's 'war' wouldn't be easy for the rest of us to ignore.

At Nets Azzie told us that Griffiths Hall had smashed his dad's team. "Dad's XI got 62 for five, but Griffiths Hall knocked them off in 14 overs and they only lost one wicket."

"I bet he's furious," said Marty.

"He pretends he's not – he keeps saying it's only a game. But he's got them all out having extra practice this morning."

"At least they did better than Wyckham," I said.

"Victor Eddy got 40 not out for the Windies," said Azzie. "That's nearly a hundred runs he's scored in two games."

"They're just too good. I expect they'll murder us, too," said Marty.

"Trust you," said Cal. "We can always count on Mr Gloomy."

"Look on the bright side, Mart," said Frankie. "We probably won't even play them."

"That's right," said Jo. "If Durbanville beat Mack's team we might not even make the semi finals." She showed us what she meant.

GROUP A

	PLAYED	WON	LOST	RUN RATE	POINTS
MACK'S ACADEMY (Aus.)	1	1	0	4.5	4
GLORY GARDENS (Eng.)	2	1	1	4.1	4
DURBANVILLE (S.A.)	1	0	1	3.7	0

GROUP B

	PLAYED	WON	LOST	RUN RATE	POINTS
Griffiths Hall (W.I.)	2	2	0	4.9	8
Wyckham (Eng.)	1	0	1	3.2	0
Mr Nazar's XI (I. & P.)	1	0	1	3.1	0

"It's all down to run rate," explained Jo.

I looked at the Group tables. "You mean if we all get four points the two with the best run rate will go through to the semis?"

"Yes, that's the rule."

"The Aussies have already got a better rate than us," said Marty.

"And that's how it's going to stay," said Mack arriving just at that moment. "How are you suckers feeling after yesterday's thrashing? Don't be too downhearted. You just met a class team."

"I don't call scraping in by two runs a thrashing," said Cal.

"Oh come on, if it hadn't been for you and Ohbert we'd have won by 40 or more."

"Then you're lucky we've got only one Ohbert," said Tylan. Ohbert heard his name and stopped talking to himself. He looked up and grinned stupidly at us. For once he wasn't wearing his Walkman and he looked a bit odd without it. He'd lent it to Brad who'd decided he'd rather listen to anything – even Ohbert's tapes – than to Ohbert and his family.

"What are you doing here anyway?" Jacky asked Mack. "It's supposed to be a Durbanville and Glory Gardens practice session. No Aussies admitted."

"I just thought I'd come along and give you some extra coaching," said Mack. "I noticed a small weakness against left-arm spin for a start."

We let him stay because Marty said he wanted a chance to bowl flat out at him.

Kiddo started Nets with 'some useful tips for batters'. The others complain that Kiddo drones on too much at Nets and to tell the truth he can be pretty boring, but I usually listen to him because now and again he says something useful.

"Never do what the bowler wants you to do," Kiddo began. "If he sets a field with three slips and a gully, it probably means he wants you to cover drive. If he has two fielders on the long-leg boundary, he wants you to hook. Look at the field closely, sort out where the fielders are – especially the good ones – and try and outwit him."

"What if the hook's your favourite shot?" asked Clive.

"Then play it. But if you know you usually hook in the air, think about the chances of giving a catch. I always look at the field and rehearse two things in my mind."

"That's one too many for you, Ohbert," said Frankie.

"Frankie, must you always interrupt with your silly comments?" said Kiddo.

"Sorry, Prof," said Frankie, winking at Cal.

Kiddo gave Frankie an icy look and then carried on.

"First," he said, "I ask myself, where are the gaps in the field? And second, what are my best shots? Use the range of shots you know you can play – always work with what you have. My favourite shot is the cover drive – so I'm going to play it even if there are five slips. But if the ball's cutting or swinging away outside the off-stump I'll probably leave it alone. A good player will always have time to change his mind at the last split second."

Then he showed us how to control an attacking shot like a pull off the back foot. Azzie picked it up instantly.

Azzie uses the full width of the crease to play this pull shot. He rocks back on his right foot, ready to hit the ball in front of square. First he's on his toes to get on top of the ball and as he plays the shot he's perfectly balanced. That means he can adjust his shot at the last minute and reduce power or defend if necessary. Notice the follow through: eye on the ball and weight on the left foot.

We all practised playing short-pitched deliveries. Frankie bowled a slow full toss at Joe and he pulled it off the middle of the bat. The ball disappeared in a shower of spray and sticky bits.

"A peach of a ball," laughed Frankie as Joe picked the lumps of fruit out of his shirt and hair.

"Frankie, where'd you find that peach?" asked Mack.

"In the changing room somewhere."

"I thought so. You nicked it from my lunch box, didn't you?"

"You've just pulled Mack's lunch for four, Joe," said Frankie and he turned to Mack. "Sorry. He's got no respect for other people's food."

We finished the session with some fielding practice. One good way of building up your fitness is a practice game called 'decking the catcher'. The catcher stands in the middle of three or four throwers who stand about two or three metres away from him. The idea is to keep the catcher on the floor by throwing catch after catch, forcing him to dive for the ball each time. As he catches it, he must throw it straight back to one of the throwers who then throws him another catch before he can get to his feet.

After Nets Frankie announced the closing entries for the Sausage Eating World Championship. It was still just the four contenders: Thompson Gale (W.I.), Kipper Hawkes (Aus.), Joe Reddy (S.A.) and Frankie Allen (Eng.). Frankie tried to get Ohbert to enter as the extra-terrestrial contender but Ohbert said he didn't like sausages much. "Next time can we have a baked potato competition?" he asked.

Brad Miller groaned. "Not baked potatoes! That's all they ever eat in his house." It was the first time Brad had spoken for days.

"Oh but, I like baked potatoes."

"So did I once," said Brad sadly. He was looking paler and paler every day and I began to wonder if he would survive the fortnight.

Frankie went through the rules for the contest. "We'll each start with ten jumbo hot dogs. The first to finish them all will be the winner."

"What if you can't eat them all?" asked Cal.

"Seems unlikely." Frankie thought for a moment. "Well then it'll be the one who's eaten the most after 15 minutes. And I'll have the left overs."

"Have you told Thompson and Kipper?" asked Mack.

"Don't worry, I've organised everything," said Frankie.

"This I must see," said Cal.

"You just wait," he said. "I've told everyone it will be in the home changing room tomorrow after the Acks v Durbanville game. Thompson's bringing a stop watch, I've got the plates. What else is there?"

"Sausages?" suggested Jo.

"Oh yes, I forgot about them," said Frankie. "I wonder where I can get 40 hot dogs."

Chapter Nine

When Cal, Marty, Frankie and I finally arrived at the Priory, the match between Mack's Acks and Durbanville was well into its second innings.

I can't remember why we were so late. I think we might have got in a muddle about the time that the game started. Jo said it was Frankie's fault and she was probably right. She'd been scoring for Durbanville and she told us that they had held the Acks to 69 for eight off their 20 overs.

"So who's winning?" asked Frankie.

"We *were*," said Joe. "But we've just lost three wickets for two runs. Louis went and ran himself out. And Johnny Malan got a duck."

"I bet it had a loud quack," said Cal.

"What's happening with the run rate," I asked Jo. If we were still behind Mack's team after their innings our chances of qualifying for the semi-final would be pretty slim.

"I haven't had time to work it out yet but it must be close," said Jo. "If you score for me I'll soon tell you. Make sure you do it in pencil though – in case you make a mistake."

Another wicket fell and Joe got up to bat. Stuck right in the middle of his back was a large message which read I'M AN IDIOT. SHAKE HANDS WITH ME IF YOU AGREE. Frankie's writing, of course.

Joe didn't have the faintest idea what all the laughter was about. He made his way out to the middle, all the time looking around to see what the joke was. Each fielder shook hands with him as he passed.

"I'd heard you lot were friendly but this is ridiculous," said Joe to Mack.

"It's just an old Australian custom," said Mack shaking hands firmly. "Specially when you meet a dingbat."

"What's a dingbat?"

"Someone with a kangaroo loose in the top field."

"Er . . . I think I get the message," said Joe.

"I don't think so," spluttered Sam, the wicket-keeper.

Joe got off the mark with two leg byes from a no ball. I looked at the score-book. Did the two go in the no ball column or the leg byes? It couldn't be both because that would add up to four. "Help!" I said to Jo.

"It goes down as two no balls unless the batsman hits it. If it had come off the bat, it would have been 2 runs to Joe," said Jo. "You show it in the bowler's analysis like this."

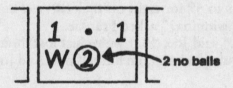

I did as I was told. Suddenly Jo looked up and smiled, "Hurray, we're through, Hooker. We're in the semi-finals."

"Are you sure?"

"Yes, look. I've double checked it."

I peered at Jo's sums.

	POINTS	RUN RATE
Glory Gardens (Eng.)	4	4.092
Mack's Academy (Aus.)	4	3.975
Durbanville (S.A.)	0	?

"Umm, what does it mean?" I asked.

"We've got a better run rate than Mack's team – only by a fraction, but it's enough. Durbanville can still beat us if they win this game in 15.5 overs or less. But it means that we must qualify."

"I see," I said, lying through my teeth. "But what if the Acks win?"

"Don't be a dumbo. That means they get 8 points, we get 4 and Durbanville 0 – so obviously we still go through."

"I'll take your word for it."

"Oh, give me the score-book," said Jo. "You've just missed a run."

"We're through to the next round," I told the others.

"How come?" asked Cal.

"On run rate." I hoped he wouldn't ask me to explain it. All I knew was that if Durbanville won, either they or the Acks would go out on a slower scoring rate.

Joe was now peppering the Australian bowling all over the Priory. He'd already scored 20 and he'd only been in for ten minutes, although he'd been dropped twice. Each time he scored a run someone would come up and shake his hand.

"They're so sporting, these Australians," laughed Frankie.

"I think that sign's bringing him luck," said Azzie.

"Perhaps he should wear it all the time – or have it tattooed on his back," said Frankie chuckling.

The score had rocketed up to 56 when Joe was clean bowled by the Kipper. He walked back to the pavilion, shaking hands as he went.

"Funny people these Australians," he said, sitting down next to Frankie. "Good knock, though?"

"Not bad for an idiot," said Frankie. "I've got to hand it to you Joe, you put your back into your batting."

Two more wickets fell on 56 and the scoring rate slowed almost to a standstill. I told Louis that they needed to get the runs quickly. "Jo says you've got to score them in 16 overs and 1 ball to qualify ahead of the Acks."

"I know, she told me, too." The fifteenth over was just

beginning and Durbanville still needed ten to win.

Mack had got the message, too. He had his field set right out on the boundary. Only four runs came off the first four balls, then a two and another single. The fielding was brilliant. Even Kipper managed to bend down and stop an off-drive that was whistling away to the boundary.

Louis watched calmly while Johnny Malan boomed instructions from the boundary edge. "Four, four, hit it for four. Get down the track to it, you fool," he hollered at poor Brad Miller. I really felt sorry for him; first he has to live with Ohbert and now the whole team was depending on him to knock the winning runs against the clock.

"Come on Brad, we're dozing off," shouted Johnny. "Hit it man."

"This is it," said Louis quietly.

Brad faced the first ball of the sixteenth over needing three to win. Mack was the bowler. He dropped the ball right in the block hole. Brad swung and missed.

"Useless," boomed Johnny.

Louis put his head in his hands. Durbanville won the match with a four off the next ball, finishing on 71 for seven. But it wasn't quite good enough to qualify. Jo's table shows why.

	P	W	L	Pts	R/R
Glory Gardens (Eng.)	2	1	1	4	4.092
Mack's Academy (Aus.)	2	1	1	4	3.975
Durbanville Darts (S.A.)	2	1	1	4	3.963

"Knocked out by a hundredth of a run," moaned Joe.

"That means Mack's Acks play the West Indies," said Jacky.

Brad walked in looking pale and dejected. Louis slapped him on the back. "Well done," he said. "It was my fault we didn't qualify, not yours."

"Oh but . . . well batted, Brad," said Ohbert rushing up to his hero. Brad sighed heavily and looked for his Walkman.

And who do we play? I wondered. It wasn't long before we knew the answer. Azzie's dad arrived in his new Peugeot and he was looking dead pleased with himself. His team had beaten Wyckham by 11 runs. So this was how the group B table finished:

	P	W	L	Pts
Griffiths Hall (W.I.)	2	2	0	8
Mr Nazar's X1 (I. & P.)	2	1	1	4
Wyckham (Eng.)	2	0	2	0

"No points for Wyckham!" said Frankie. "Wait till I see Katzy."

Jo pinned up the draw for the semi-finals on the Priory notice board.

WORLD CUP SEMI-FINALS

Wednesday, August 10th
2pm. Eastgate Priory ground:
Glory Gardens v Mr Nazar's XI

2.30pm. Wyckham Wanderers ground:
Mack's Academy v Griffiths Hall School

We were all so excited that we completely forgot about Frankie's competition. I think Frankie had, too – until Tylan's dad arrived with the sausages.

"Where do you want them, Frankie?" he asked.

"In the changing room, please," said Frankie.

"You fat scrounger," said Tylan. "How did you manage that?"

Frankie smiled.

Tylan's dad runs the famous 'knicker stall' in the market. We all take turns to work for him on Saturdays to earn money for the club. And there's a hot dog and burger bar right next to his stall.

"I just mentioned that we'd be really hungry after the game and he sort of volunteered," said Frankie. "After all he is sort of our main sponsor, isn't he?"

"Perhaps we should have 'Knicker Stall' printed on our cricket shirts," suggested Cal.

There were tons of hot dogs, plenty for everyone.

Joe and Frankie arranged the biggest ones on four plates in the changing room. There were ten on each plate. "Real gutbusters, aren't they?" said Joe – he was still wearing his 'idiot' sign.

We had to wait for a bit for Thompson Gale and his West Indian supporters to turn up, but finally we all squeezed into the changing room – almost four cricket teams in a space only just big enough for one.

Thompson Gale got off to a flier. Four of the hot dogs on his plate vanished in seconds. Then suddenly he started to cough and choke. "Water. Quick water!" he gasped.

Joe started laughing. He laughed so much that a mouthful of sausage went up his nose and he started choking, too.

Frankie took the lead. But my money was on Kipper. He was steadily munching his way through everything on his plate. Frankie slowed and then stuck on his eighth hot dog but Kipper ploughed on. His glasses steamed up but he didn't slow down – nine, nine and a half, ten.

"The Kipper wins," cried Mack and the Aussies cheered and tried in vain to hoist Kipper on their shoulders. They all collapsed in a heap in the middle of the crowded changing room. Frankie was on his ninth sausage; Thompson had stuck on five and Joe had managed only four.

"What happened to you?" Frankie asked Joe through a mouthful of sausage. "You were pathetic."

"Thompson ate your sausages," chuckled Joe. "At least they were meant for you. I covered them in hot chilli sauce."

"I know, I saw you fix them. I switched plates with you when you weren't looking, only Thompson sat in your place by mistake."

Thompson was still gasping for breath and wiping the sweat from his forehead.

"You'd better not tell him," said Joe. "He might be bowling against you in the final."

"Pity I didn't give them to Kipper," said Frankie. "Then I'd have won."

Ohbert had watched the whole event with a mixture of delight and puzzlement. As usual, he didn't know what was going on but, without his Walkman, he was forced to pay attention for a change.

"I bet you could have beaten Kipper, Ohbert," said Frankie.

Ohbert grinned and looked at Joe. "Why have you got that sign on your back?" he asked.

Chapter Ten

Wednesday came round so quickly I hardly had time to think about the team. There wasn't much to think about anyway. It was the same eleven – I just had my fingers crossed that no one got sick.

(in batting order)	Hooker Knight
Matthew Rose	Frankie Allen
Cal Sebastien	Tylan Vellacott
Azzie Nazar	Jacky Gunn
Clive da Costa	Marty Lear
Erica Davies	Ohbert Bennett

I knew Louis was disappointed to miss out on the World Cup semi-finals but he didn't let on. I've never met anyone quite so calm and cool about things as Louis. He told me that all the Durbanville players (with the exception of Brad) were having the time of their lives and they'd come and support us in the semis and the final. *And*, he said, Glory Gardens was going to win the World Cup and when Louis said something like that he made you believe it.

Kiddo organised a friendly for Durbanville against Wyckham on Friday to make up for them going out of the competition, so at least they would all play another game of cricket before they left.

We didn't know much at all about Mr Nazar's team. Azzie told us his dad had gone round the local clubs and schools picking some of the best players. Wyckham's ace spinner,

Yousef Mohamed, was their captain. He's good, he plays for the County Colts with us. I recognized one or two of the others, too, but mostly they were completely new to me.

"We'll have to give them another name," said Frankie.

"Who?"

"Azzie's old man's team. We can't go on calling them Mr Nazar's XI; it sounds like a load of geriatrics."

"Why not India & Pakistan?" said Jo.

"That's too long."

"What about Az's Dad's Team?" suggested Tylan.

"That's it – the Azdadz," Frankie grinned and pulled on one of his cricket socks. The smile faded as he watched his toes appear through the end of the sock. "Someone's cut my toe off!"

Cal laughed and held up Frankie's other sock. The toe had been snipped cleanly off that one, too. "I shouldn't worry," said Cal. "These socks are so old they'll be glad to be put out of their misery."

"Tell that to my mum. If she finds out she'll kill me," said Frankie.

"I wonder who did it?" said Tylan.

"Three guesses." Frankie pulled on his cricket shirt. It was covered in little arrows like a convict's uniform.

"You'll get arrested if you wear that," said Azzie.

"I'll wear it inside out, then," said Frankie, furiously going through all his cricket gear to see if there was any more damage. His shoes had orange toes and stapled to his cap there was a message scrawled in red ink: 'GET REDDY BEFORE HE GETS YOU!'

I won the toss and we batted. Erica had asked me if she could open the batting for a change and since Cal didn't mind going down the order after his brilliant 48, I agreed. I was pretty sure Erica wouldn't let us down. So she and Matt padded up.

"Anyone seen my sixpence?" asked Matthew.

"Your what?"

"My lucky sixpence."

"What's it look like?"

"It's an old sixpence coin – a small, silver one. I keep it in my cricket trousers when I'm batting – for luck," said Matthew going red.

"Hasn't been much use then, has it?" said Clive cruelly.

Matthew didn't reply.

"Oh but, you can borrow my lucky frog if you like," said Ohbert. He pulled a small green plastic frog out of his pocket and gave it to Matthew.

"Oh thanks, Ohbert," said Matt. He looked uncertainly at the little frog in his hand and then put it in his pocket and walked out to bat.

He and Erica put on 17 for the first wicket against some steady seam bowling although both bowlers were pitching it a bit short. Matthew got a nasty knock in the box from a quick one from the faster of the two – his name was down in the score-book as L. Sidi.

"I bet Matt's dead pleased with your frog so far, Ohbert," said Frankie. "It seems to be making him a bit jumpy."

After five overs Youz turned to spin which I'd been half expecting. Youz takes piles of wickets for the Colts and he can turn the ball both ways. But it was the left-armer from the top end who caught my eye. He was bowling quite quickly for a spinner and there wasn't much time to adjust when the ball turned off the pitch. He beat Matthew a couple of times outside the off-stump and then he completely deceived Erica with a slower one which she went to play on the leg side and got a leading edge. The ball lobbed up for an easy return catch to the bowler.

"Well bowled, Kiran. Great ball," shouted Youz rushing up to congratulate his bowler.

Azzie went off like a train. He danced down the pitch to the captain and carved him through extra-cover to the boundary. Then he cut the left-armer hard for another four. We were really beginning to pull it together when Matt pushed one wide of gully and called for a quick single. He simply couldn't have picked up the fielder lurking behind at point. Suddenly the ball was in the fielder's hands and he crashed down the stumps at the batter's end with a perfect direct throw. Azzie lunged to slide his bat in but he was well short. He didn't even bother to look at the umpire but carried on running in the direction of the pavilion.

"That's twice in a row he's been run out," I said.

"He needs sharpening up," said Frankie. "Leave him to me."

This is how the left-arm spinner gets his rhythm. His run up is between the umpire and the stumps and as close to the wicket as possible. Again it's important to learn to spin the ball hard. The index finger and middle finger are stretched across the seam and as the ball is released you flick the wrist hard in a forward anti-clockwise direction. That will give the ball bounce and spin it away to the slips.

"The Frankie Allen speed training course – you must tell me more," laughed Cal.

Once again Clive went in to bat as we were under a bit of pressure. I think he prefers to get his eye in against the quickies rather than against spin. Of course, he'll tell you he's a great player of spin. But it seems to me he's more at ease against the quick stuff at the beginning of his innings. This time he tried an ambitious sweep shot too early on and dragged the ball straight into his stumps.

"At least he can't say he wasn't out this time," said Jacky.

"Want to bet?" said Frankie mischievously.

In came Cal – the player in form. Like Azzie and Clive he decided to take the attack to the bowlers. He pulled a short one from Kiran, the left-armer, to the leg-side boundary. It bounced over the rope and hit Gatting on the nose. He woke up with a yelp and waddled off to lick his wound in his den under the pavilion steps.

Cal shaped to drive the next ball. He got a thick edge behind cover point and ran the first one fast. "Two," he shouted as they crossed. Matthew turned. He looked up at the fielder who had just reached the ball and hesitated. "Wait," he said, but it was too late – by now Cal was half way down the track. He stopped. Matthew suddenly realised the danger and started to run. Cal turned. Matthew stopped. The fielder spotted his chance and sent in a low, skimming throw to the bowler. Cal dived for the line but he wasn't even in the race.

"Idiot!" he screamed, furiously turning on Matthew. "Are you planning to run out the whole team?"

Matt looked miserable, "Sorry, Cal. I should . . ."

"Sorry, Cal," mimicked Cal. He stormed off, now and again looking back and glaring at Matthew.

I got up and pulled on my batting gloves. As I walked towards Cal I could see he was shaking with rage. His eyes looked wild. "Tell him when he gets out I'm waiting for him," he snarled as we passed each other. I said nothing. Cal's got a terrible temper but it never lasts long. At times like this it's best to leave him alone and let him cool down.

I glanced at the score-board before walking to the wicket. 43 for four. Matthew had scored 10 of them and the last thing I wanted was for him to throw his wicket away because of two silly run outs. I called him over. "Forget about it and get your head down," I said.

It was doubly unfortunate that I managed to run myself out going for a quick single. I'd just got off the mark with a two. Then I pushed one into the covers and ran. It was my call and I thought I was in easily, but that wasn't how the umpire saw it. I was cross – my batting had been a disaster throughout the World Cup; my scores had been 2, 4 and 2 and the last thing I needed was a lousy run out decision.

It definitely wasn't Matt's fault anyway. But I couldn't convince Cal and Clive of that.

"That's three people he's run out!" said Clive.

"When will he be happy? When he's got a world record?" said Cal but I could see he'd already calmed down a lot.

Frankie was next in. He faced two balls from Kiran, the left-armer. The first Frankie tried to swing away to square-leg and it straightened on him. There was a huge appeal for lbw. "Not out," said old Sid and Frankie at the same time.

Then Kiran bowled a beauty which bounced and lifted outside the off-stump. Frankie went through with his swing and again the slips and keeper went up. "Owzthat!" This time Sid raised his finger.

"What!" said Frankie, amazed. He turned and walked off rubbing his shoulder.

"Don't be daft, it hit your bat," shouted the wicket-keeper.

Frankie turned round. "Do you want to see the bruise on my shoulder?"

"No way. I heard the snick."

"Are you calling me a cheat?" said Frankie.

The keeper shrugged. "Umpire's decision," he said.

Frankie joined the growing number of discontented Glory

Gardens players on the boundary. "It's time old Sid had his eyes and ears tested," he said.

"He probably thought you'd already lost one life with that lbw," said Marty.

"And at least he saved you from being run out by Matthew," said Cal.

"Just look at him," said Clive who always enjoys having a go at Matt for scoring slowly. "He's crawling along at under a run an over and he's already cost us three of our best wickets."

Tylan had to face the opening bowler, Rai Singh, who came back on at the canal end. Ty doesn't have much of a clue how to play quick stuff but he got behind the ball and he stuck at it even though he got hit twice – on the arm and on the thigh.

At last Matthew started to open up. He played a sweet off-drive for two followed by a delicate leg glance. I looked at the board – 55 for seven – but it came as a shock to see that we only had five overs left.

Jacky was padded up to go in next. "We need to go for it," I said to him. "Seven or eight an over." As I spoke Tylan looped a simple catch to mid-on.

Jacky got up. "I'll see if I can get Matthew moving," he said.

It was L. Sidi who had taken the wicket. Youz had brought him back to bowl his last two overs. Jacky edged his first ball only inches wide of the keeper and then slogged one back just over the bowler's head.

"El Sidi's not happy about that," said Frankie. "Bet you a quid the next one's a bouncer."

No one took the bet – and a bouncer it was. The bowler dug it in short and it reared up and hit Jacky on the chest. Jacky took two steps down the track, threw down his bat and glared at the bowler. "Just wait till you bat," he said. "You're dead!"

Old Sid told him to calm down but he also had a quiet word with the bowler.

All this seemed to wake Matthew up. He suddenly launched into the bowling and hit two cracking drives. The second went soaring over mid-off.

"It went in the air," gasped Clive.

"It can't have, it's Matthew," said Frankie.

"I bet he can't do it again." Cal had hardly finished speaking when a savage pull cleared square-leg and bounced into the fence.

"Wow," whistled Cal. "Another one of those and I might even forgive him."

With two overs remaining we were on 72 for seven and Matthew's total had raced to 27. In the next over Jacky was stumped, swinging at a ball after taking a walk half way down the wicket. If he'd connected it would have cleared the canal.

Matthew and Marty hustled eight off the first five balls of the last over, thanks to some extraordinary running between the wickets.

"I think they're both trying to run each other out," said Tylan.

"Wouldn't surprise me," said Cal.

It was Matthew who faced up to the last ball of the innings. He cracked it hard in the air straight at cover point who couldn't hang on to the catch. It burst through his fingers and deflected into his face. Marty and Matthew ran two and the innings ended: 85 for eight. The cover point fielder was helped off with blood running down his nose and I went over to see if he was all right.

Matthew had made 39 and even his two run-out victims cheered him in.

"Sorry about the . . ." began Matthew.

"Forget it," said Cal.

"You did the right thing," said Azzie.

"What?"

"Stayed out there until Cal cooled down."

"Oh but, Matthew," said Ohbert.

"Yes?"

"Would you like to keep my frog?"

"I think I would, Ohbert," smiled Matthew.

HOME TEAM	GLORY GARDENS	V	MR NAZAR'S XI	AWAY TEAM	AT EASTGATE PRIORY
					DATE AUG 10

INNINGS OF GLORY GARDENS .... TOSS WON BY G.G. WEATHER SUNNY

BATSMAN	RUNS SCORED	HOW OUT	BOWLER	SCORE
1 M. ROSE	·1·2·1·1·1·1·2·1·2·2·1·1·2·3(29) 4·1·2·1·2·2·3·1·2	NOT	OUT	39
2 E. DAVIES	·1·1·2·1·1·2	c k b	BHARATKUMAR	8
3 A. NAZAR	4·1·4·2·1	RUN	OUT	12
4 C. DA COSTA	2·	bowled	BHARATKUMAR	2
5 C. SEBASTIEN	4·2	RUN	OUT	6
6 H. KNIGHT	2·	RUN	OUT	2
7 F. ALLEN	·	ct PATIL	BHARATKUMAR	0
8 T. VELLACOTT	1·	ct GOPALAN	SIDI	1
9 J. GUNN	1·1·1·1·	st PATIL	BUTT	5
10 M. LEAR	1·	NOT	OUT	1
11				

FALL OF WICKETS

	1	2	3	4	5	6	7	8	9	10
SCORE	18	30	34	43	47	47	55	75		
BAT NO	1	3	4	5	6	7	8	9		

BYES	1·	2	TOTAL EXTRAS 9
LEG BYES	1·1·1·	4	TOTAL FOR 85
WIDES	1·	1	WKTS 8
NO BALLS	1·1	2	

SCORE AT A GLANCE

BOWLING ANALYSIS ⊙ NO BALL + WIDE

BOWLER	1	2	3	4	5	6	7	8	9	10	11	12	13	OVS	MDS	RUNS	WKT
1 R. SINGH	1·· ··	··2 ·2·	X	·2· +·	X									4	0	10	0
2 L. SIDI	2·· ·1·	·1· 1·1	X	1·1 ·w	X									4	0	16	1
3 YOUSEF MOHAMED	··⊙1 ·1·	··w ·1·	M	2·· 2·	X									4	1	11	0
4 K. BHARATKUMAR	··w ·1·w	·w 2·1	1·2 w·	2·1 ··w	X									4	0	18	3
5 V. BUTT	21· ·1·	1·2 7·1	·2· 1w·											3	0	14	1
6 S. GOPALAN	222 112													1	0	10	0
7																	
8																	
9																	

Chapter Eleven

I was half expecting it when Kiddo walked into our changing room and shut the door. He hates it when you complain about the opposition or criticise the umpire's decisions.

"What's niggling you lot, today?" he said.

Silence.

"Here comes a lecture," whispered Frankie in my ear. Kiddo's famous for his long speeches about sportsmanship and 'playing the game'. But for once he surprised us. "Any more of it and you're disqualified," he said quietly. And he walked out.

"What was all that about?" said Frankie.

"Anyone's guess," said Clive.

But I knew what Kiddo was talking about. Frankie and Cal were laughing and joking again; they'd completely forgotten about the things they'd said. But Jacky was sitting, scowling in his corner of the changing room – he'd still got El Sidi's bouncer on his mind.

Before we went out to field I looked in at the opposition's changing room to see if the player Matthew had hit was okay. His nose was purple but it had stopped bleeding and he said it felt fine. Youz said he thought Matthew had batted really well under pressure.

Jacky was so fired up at the beginning of the Azdadz innings that he bowled faster even than Marty. But it was Marty who took the first wicket. He found a bit of extra bite and the ball took the shoulder of the bat and lobbed to me in the gully. It was an easy catch but I did a dive after I'd caught it to make it look more difficult – just for Frankie's sake.

"Marvellous," said Frankie. "Best impersonation of Gatting I've ever seen."

The fall of the first wicket brought El Sidi to the middle and Jacky's eyes lit up. He took the ball from Frankie at the beginning of his second over. "This one's mine."

The first ball was a quick bouncer and the batsman ducked. The next was also short but this time El Sidi stepped inside it and hooked it for two. Jacky glared at him and walked back to his mark. Another shortish delivery reared up and hit the batsman's glove but he managed to play it down in front of him. Old Sid spoke to Jacky as he walked back to his mark. "Pitch it up, laddy," he said.

Now for the yorker if he's got any sense, I thought. Even when he's mad Jacky's a thinking bowler and a fast straight yorker hammered into El Sidi's toe. He jumped in the air as it hit him. Jacky swung round with both arms raised and appealed to Sid, "OWZTHAT!" Sid raised his finger. Jacky turned on El Sidi and pointed to the pavilion.

That's enough, I thought and I quickly rushed up to Jacky before he said anything he'd regret. "Well bowled. Now cool it. We don't want to be disqualified."

"Well he's a . . ." began Jacky.

"Just keep your strength for your bowling."

"Here comes Captain Sensible," Cal said to me as I walked back to gully.

With the last ball of his over Jacky clean bowled the other opener and the Azdadz were struggling on 11 for three. We gave Jacky a round of applause as he walked down to long-leg at the end of the over. He didn't say anything but he was looking pretty pleased with life again.

Marty and Jacky bowled out their spells without taking another wicket. Marty tried every tactic he knew: changing the angle, varying his flight, going round the wicket – anything to unsettle the batsmen.

Marty goes round the wicket to present the batsman with a new direction and a different set of problems. Look how wide of the crease he is bowling on this occasion. When he bowls over the wicket he usually comes through very close to the stumps.

Both batsmen, Youz and Sunil Gopalan, only survived by the skin of their teeth and a good bit of luck. Marty dropped a difficult catch and bowled low down by his right ankle and old Sid turned down another loud shout for lbw from Jacky.

I decided to go for an all spin attack with Tylan and Cal. Unfortunately it wasn't one of Tylan's 'on' days. He started badly with a horrible long hop which was pulled for four – and things got steadily worse. His first over went for ten runs but he kept most of the rubbish for the second. He bowled two wides down the leg side and a couple more terrible long hops were dispatched for four by Youz. Twelve runs came off the over and, of course, I took him off. But the damage had been done. In the course of three overs the Azdadz had gone from being out of the game to 53 for three, and they were less than half way through their twenty overs.

I decided to bring on Erica. She is always economical but it was asking a lot – even of her – to keep the scoring rate below three an over. What we needed most of all now were wickets.

In his next over Cal found the answer. He'd been bowling a tight off-stump line and keeping the batsmen on the defensive. "Can I have a short mid-wicket?" he asked me.

"What for? We've got to keep the runs down."

"I know, but this one keeps flicking me off his legs. If I pitch it up to him on leg stump he might knock it in the air."

"I'll try a 6:3 field – but no loose ones outside the off-stump, mind."

"Okay."

So this was the rather strange field I set for Cal.

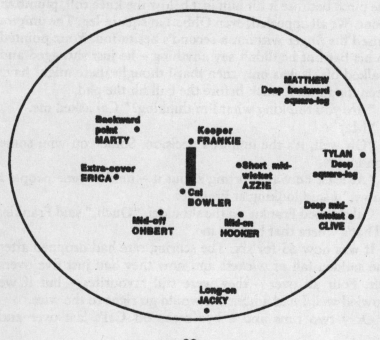

And, believe it or not, it worked. The second ball of the over flew in the air straight to Azzie at short mid-wicket and he snapped it up. Cal grinned, "Simple game, cricket, isn't it?"

"Have you any more brilliant ideas?" I asked.

"As soon as I think of one I'll let you know. But don't count on it."

Three balls later Cal took another wicket. He bowled his slower ball and the batsman just tapped it back to him. It was like catching practice.

But Youz was still there and that worried me. He was looking well on top of the bowling and while he was at the wicket the odds were always stacked against us. Erica was keeping the ball well-pitched-up to him, encouraging him to go for the drive. He hit her for two down to long-on. She held back the next for a fraction; it was just short of a length and Youz went only half forward to it. It must have nipped in off the pitch because it hit him just below the knee roll, plumb in front. We all appealed, even Ohbert at square-leg. The umpire raised his finger without a second's hesitation. Youz pointed to his bat but he didn't say anything – he just shrugged and walked off. It was only then that I thought there might have been the faintest snick before the ball hit the pad.

"Are you thinking what I'm thinking?" Cal asked me.

"Maybe."

"Oh well, it's the umpire's decision. Some you win; some you lose."

"At least he was sporting about it – unlike some people I know," I said looking at Frankie.

Cal slapped Frankie on the shoulder, "Ouch," said Frankie. "That's where that ball hit me."

It was now 65 for six. The scoring rate had dropped after the sudden fall of wickets and now they had just five overs left. Four an over – they were still favourites – but if we bowled well I had a hunch it would go right to the wire.

Only two runs and a bye came off Cal's last over and

This is the question the umpire has to ask. If the ball has taken the thinnest edge of bat on its way through to the pad, the batsman cannot be out lbw – even though he is right in front. It's one of the hardest umpiring decisions because it's often very difficult to distinguish between the two sounds of the ball hitting bat and pad – particularly if they are close together like this.

Frankie dropped a fairly easy catch, too. Cal finished his spell with two for 12. The new batsmen were not timing the ball well yet and I took a gamble on them not hitting clean boundaries and brought the field in slightly to cut off the singles. My luck held and Erica's next over cost only three.

Someone had to bowl the last two overs at Cal's end and I decided it had better be me. They now needed exactly five an over off the last three. I kept the field in – forcing them to try and hit it over the top. One wild swing cleared Tylan at square-leg but then Cal took a finger-tip catch at mid-wicket to even the odds again. No one else in the team would have been tall enough to reach it. They still took five off my first over. 75 for seven with 12 balls left.

I changed the field again for Erica. She wanted to bowl an off-stump line and so I gave her five fielders on the off-side and four on the on. It takes some nerve to do that with tailenders who usually swing away to leg whatever the line – but Erica kept them guessing with variations of pace and length.

After her third ball I heard her turn to the umpire and ask how many balls there were left in the over. I knew that was a signal to Frankie. It meant she was going to bowl a slow delivery. Frankie crept up to the stumps as she ran in. It was a flighted, slow leg break and it had the batsman groping well out of his crease. He got a big surprise when he turned round to see Frankie appealing for the stumping and grinning all over his face. The plan had worked; he was out.

As the last over began the Azdadz were 78 for eight. With eight needed I just had to stop the twos and boundaries. I had four fielders half way back and five on the boundary. My first ball was right in the block hole. Frankie rushed round from behind the stumps and prevented a single. The next was a slog down to Jacky for one, although he nearly gave away overthrows with a wild throw, way over Frankie's head. Fortunately Marty sprinted round and managed to stop it with a brilliant dive. With seven to get off four balls they now really needed to take risks. I pushed the field back further to prevent the boundary attempt – one four and they'd be back in the game. Off the next ball they tried to run two to Azzie at deep mid-wicket. He attacked the ball and his throw was spot on. Frankie flicked off the bails to complete a smart run out. The fourth ball of my over was straight and it took out middle stump. They were all out for 80.

"West Indies, here we come," cried Frankie, pulling up a stump and waving it over his head as he charged towards the pavilion.

Azzie's dad, Youz and the rest of the Azdadz were standing in front of the pavilion to clap us in.

"Well played," said Mr Nazar as I shook hands with Youz.

"Well bowled, Glory Gardens," boomed the voice of Johnny Malan.

"Anyone know how the other game went?" asked Cal.

"It's no contest. The West Indies'll stuff the Acks," said Frankie.

"I wouldn't be too sure," said Cal.

"Bet you a strawberry, chocolate and vanilla ice-cream," said Frankie.

"You're on."

We set off for Wyckham's ground with Kiddo and Azzie's dad to find out the result. The Durbanville bus followed on behind.

INNINGS OF MR NAZAR'S XI.......... TOSS WON BY G.G.... WEATHER SUNNY

BATSMAN	RUNS SCORED	HOW OUT	BOWLER	SCORE
1 D. THACKERAY	2.1.1	ct KNIGHT	LEAR	4
2 SALEED IBRAHIM	2	bowled	GUNN	2
3 L. SIDI	1.2	lbw	GUNN	3
4 YOUSEF MOHAMED	1.1.2.1.4.2.3.1.2.4.2.4.2.2 1.2	lbw	DAVIES	34
5 S. GOPALAN	2.1.3.1.1.2.2	ct NAZAR	SEBASTIEN	12
6 V. BUTT	1.	c k b	SEBASTIEN	1
7 K. BHARATKUMAR	1.1.2.1	ct SEBASTIEN	KNIGHT	5
8 R. D'SOUZA	2.1.2	st ALLEN	DAVIES	5
9 S. PATIL	1	RUN	OUT	1
10 R. SINGH	1.1	NOT	OUT	2
11 FAROUK AHMED		bowled	KNIGHT	0

FALL OF WICKETS

OVERS	2.1.1.1.		5	TOTAL EXTRAS	11

SCORE	5	8	11	61	63	65	75	77	80	80
BAT NO	1	3	2	5	6	4	7	8	9	11

BYES	2.1.1.1.	5	TOTAL EXTRAS	11
LEG BYES	2	1	TOTAL FOR	80
WIDES	1.1.1	3		
NO BALLS	1.	1	WKTS	10

SCORE AT A GLANCE

BOWLER	BOWLING ANALYSIS ⊙ NO BALL + WIDE													OVS	MDS	RUNS	WKT
	1	2	3	4	5	6	7	8	9	10	11	12	13				
1 M. LEAR														4	0	9	1
2 J. GUNN														4	0	13	2
3 T. VELLACOTT														2	0	22	0
4 C. SEBASTIEN														4	0	12	2
5 E. DAVIES														4	0	12	2
6 H. KNIGHT														1.4	0	5	2
7																	
8																	
9																	

Chapter Twelve

C al was right. The Acks *were* putting up a real
fight.

When we got to the Wyckham ground there were three
overs to go and everyone was on the edge of their seats.
Griffiths Hall had scored 128 for five off their 20 overs. But
Mack's team were going down fighting. They had scored 98
for eight. With three overs to go, they still needed ten an over
which was pretty hopeless against this quality of bowling.
Mack was batting with Kipper – so the running between the
wicket wasn't too brilliant either.

"Mack will have to do it in boundaries," said Cal. "There's
no way Kipper's going to run 30."

"Where's Thompson?" asked Frankie, looking round the
field.

"He's sick."

"I bet it was the chilli," laughed Joe.

Suddenly Kipper hit a huge six over long-on.

"That makes it interesting," said Jo.

She was right. Somehow Mack and Kipper kept up with the
rate. When the last over began they needed just 11 to win.
Richard Wallace was brought back to bowl it, but even that
didn't seem to bother them. When you're seeing the ball well
the faster it's bowled the quicker it goes off the bat. Kipper cut
the first ball away for four. But then he was out going for a
single that even Mack would have struggled to make. Kipper
didn't get half way down the track before Henderson Springer

took off the bails. Mack knocked two twos but then lost the strike for the last ball. They still needed two to win. Their No. 11, Bazza Woolf, had to face Richard for the first time. He took a huge swing at a very quick delivery, dead on line and managed to get an edge but it ran straight to third-man and they could only run a single. The scores finished level on 128. It was only the second tie I'd ever seen.

"What happens now?" I asked Kiddo.

"A single stump competition, kiddo."

"What's that?"

"Each team throws at one stump and whichever gets the most hits wins."

"You mean everyone in the side has one throw?"

"Yes, that's what we agreed. Although I don't think anyone was expecting a tie really."

Mack looked knackered; he'd scored 34. And, although he must have been gutted that they hadn't won the game outright, you'd have never guessed it.

"I'm glad you lot saw the end," he said. "You'd have never believed me otherwise. Kipper was brilliant, wasn't he?"

"So were you," said Jo.

"See you in the final," Mack winked and went off to organise his team.

Kiddo helped the Wyckham groundsman to organise the throwing competition. They planted a stump in the outfield and then arranged the boundary rope in a circle around it – about 15 metres away.

"Line up, kiddoes. One throw each." He tossed a coin and Mack won, so the Acks went first.

Mack led the way with a perfect throw that knocked the stump clean out of the ground. Then it was Griffiths Hall's turn and Richard Wallace missed by inches. They carried on, with each team taking turns to throw – some threw overarm, some underarm.

"It isn't as easy as it looks," said Frankie as he watched the fourth West Indian miss the stump.

"You couldn't hit it once in a hundred," said joe.

"Bet you a burger I can beat you," said Frankie.

"You haven't forgotten my ice-cream have you, fat man?" asked Cal.

"You haven't won it yet," said Frankie. But at that moment Cheryl Bardsley's throw just snicked the top of the stump and the Acks went two up. Victor Eddy scored his team's first hit and they were down to the last four throws. When Roz Bardsley missed for the Acks her sister hissed, "I should have thrown again instead of you. No one would have known."

While the twins were still arguing the West Indies scored another hit and it was two all. Kipper Hawkes steadied himself for his team's final throw; he missed by a whisker. So it was all down to the last player from Griffiths Hall. Their wicket-keeper, Henderson Springer stepped up – if he missed, it would be a sudden death play-off. But if he hit . . . We held our breath. He lobbed the ball underarm at the stump and it struck half way up. The West Indians all rushed forward cheering and Ohbert got tangled up in the scrum. He didn't seem to mind, and was last seen trying to reach up to give a high five to Victor Eddy.

I felt sorry for Mack. It didn't seem a very fair way to me for his team to go out but he accepted it in a typical Mack sort of way and shook hands with all the West Indians.

"That's one big ice-cream you owe me," Frankie said to Cal, licking his lips.

Cal shrugged, "You were lucky. What about double or quits for the final?"

"Okay," said Frankie. "Who's your money on?"

"Glory Gardens, of course."

"Fair enough. Two ice-creams say the West Indians win again."

"You can't bet against your own team, Francis," said Jo.

"Why not?"

"Because we might start getting suspicious when you drop all those catches," said Azzie.

"I'd be suspicious if he caught one," said Cal.

Frankie's and Joe's single stump competition wasn't played in quite the same sporting spirit. First Joe squirted Frankie in the ear with a water pistol just as he was about to throw. Frankie retaliated with a handful of exploding caps. In the end Frankie lost – I think it was 2-1, although I wasn't really watching. I was busy talking to Cal, Azzie and Louis about Saturday's final.

It was to be a 40 overs match, so it would be the longest game that most of the team had ever played in.

"I think we need a team talk," said Cal.

"From Kiddo?" I asked.

"No, from you. You're the skipper."

Azzie agreed. "Keeping your concentration going for 40 overs is different from a 20 overs slog." That was true enough, we'd both learnt that from the Colts games.

"So what am I going to say?" The thought of a team talk didn't appeal to me much and I was beginning to panic slightly at the thought of it.

"You'll think of something," said Cal unhelpfully.

"I've got a few ideas," said Louis.

"What?"

"Tell you later."

———— • ————

The final was only four days away. It would be the last day of the Durbanville tour, too, and I suddenly thought, I'm going to miss Louis. He'd only been staying with us for a short time but already it felt as if he was part of the family.

Matthew had brought in the Gazette with the article about the World Cup in it. There was a picture of me and Louis tossing up and both looking up in the air at the coin.

"I must get a copy of that for everyone in Durbanville," said Louis.

From the Gazette. Thursday 11 August.

WORLD CUP COMES TO TOWN

Young cricketers will have only one thing on their minds on Saturday: Who is going to win the World Cup?

This World Cup is not being played at Lords or in Sydney or Calcutta but here on the town's Eastgate Priory ground. Under 13s teams from South Africa (Durbanville Darts) and the West Indies (Griffiths Hall School) have challenged our own Wyckham Wanderers and Glory Gardens, the winners of the under 13s league.

Australia and India & Pakistan are here, too. They are represented by two teams which have been selected from local players.

As the Gazette goes to print, the competition is reaching its climax. The semi-finals are Griffiths Hall School (West Indies) v Mack's Academy (Australia) and Mr Nazar's XI (India & Pakistan) v Glory Gardens (England).

Eastgate Priory is expecting one of its biggest crowds of the season on Saturday for the final. The game starts at 2pm. And, if Glory Gardens make it through the semi-finals – we hope they'll lift the World Cup for England.

Well we *had* made it and the final was going to be the hardest game of cricket we'd ever played. But Mack had shown us that the West Indies could be beaten after all. I didn't know if we could win but I was certain of one thing – it was going to be a great game.

99

Chapter Thirteen

Louis and I went to bed late on Friday. It was the last night of his stay – Durbanville were leaving immediately after the final to catch their plane home. We sat in my bedroom and talked long after everyone else in the house had gone to sleep. Durbanville had played Wyckham that evening and beaten them by 26 runs. Louis scored 34 and took two wickets, so he was pretty happy.

"What will you do if you win the toss tomorrow?" asked Louis.

"Field, I think."

"Why?"

"We're quite good at chasing and our best bet's to try and hold them to a reasonable total."

"Isn't that a bit defensive."

"Maybe. What would you do?"

"Bat. You've got a good batting side and it's a brilliant wicket. If you bat and get the runs on the board you can put them under pressure. Player by player they are probably better than you and, if you let them dominate you, you won't stand a chance."

Then we went through every one of the West Indian players and talked about their weaknesses. With his amazing memory Louis not only remembered all their names but he could tell you which batsman was left-handed, which one liked to hook and so on. And he'd only seen Griffiths Hall play one-and-a-half times!

"Victor Eddy's your main problem. But I think he's a bit loose outside off-stump; he doesn't always get his foot to the pitch. It might be worth bowling him a few wide ones early on or trying Tylan against him, turning the ball away from him."

I knew I wouldn't remember all of Louis's ideas so I wrote some of them down.

BATTING

Victor Eddy – bowl outside off-stump and get him driving.
Henderson Springer – likes to hook in the air.
Cardinal Williams – pitch it up and he'll hit in the air on the off-side – destroys short bowling.
Gary Lomas – left-hander, loves to cut and sweep – don't bowl wide of off-stump.

BOWLING

Richard Wallace – fast – can bowl inswinging yorker.
Thompson Gale – fast but bowls a bit short – watch out for slower ball.
Vaughan Tossell – leg spinner – tall, gets a lot of bounce.
Victor Eddy – little cutters bowled off a short run – play on front foot if you can.

FIELDING

Watch out for Thompson Gale's throw.
Victor Eddy and Coventry Phillips – brilliant in the covers. Coventry throws both handed.
Henderson Springer – good at leg-side stumpings when the spinner is bowling.

"They're a good side," said Louis. "But they're not unbeatable. The Aussies proved that."

"Yes. I wish Mack was playing for us."

"I wish *I* was playing for you."

It was hard to believe that tonight we'd be saying goodbye to the Durbanville players: Johnny Malan with his foghorn voice, Joe Reddy, Brad Miller (probably the only one who was looking forward to leaving) and the others . . . and, of course, Louis.

I went to sleep and dreamt about winning the World Cup with a six off the last ball.

Saturday was a beautiful day, although we missed most of the morning. It was 11 o'clock when Louis and I got up. The weather had been brilliant for the whole two weeks of the World Cup. Louis couldn't believe it. "I always thought it rained every day in Britain," he said. "And where's the fog? This is hotter than South Africa."

"I thought you were going to sleep all day," said Lizzie as we came down for breakfast.

"Just preparing for the big game," I said.

"Sleeping sounds a lot more interesting to me," she said.

"This is for you," said Louis handing a little parcel to my sister. She opened it. It was a bracelet with bits of shiny stone hanging off it. "Coral," said Louis. "We've got lots in South Africa. It's a present for letting me stay here."

"It's lovely," said Lizzie, really pleased for once.

"And this is yours, Hooker." My present was a picture of a flat-topped hill called Table Mountain. "It's not that great but my mother gave me these things to give to people in England and this is all I've got left."

"You mean *you* didn't choose this bracelet for me?" said Lizzie, looking disappointed.

"Well, not exactly . . . but I thought you'd like it better than Hooker would," said Louis nudging me.

Our late breakfast was interrupted by Cal and Johnny. "Matt's got chicken pox," said Cal. "There's no way he can play or there'll be an epidemic."

"Which will spread round the world when we leave," said Johnny.

"He probably caught it from Ohbert's frog," said Cal.

"Don't be stupid, you can't get chicken pox from a frog," said Johnny.

"So *who's* going to play?" I asked.

102

"Take your pick," said Cal.

"What do you mean?"

"Well, there's no shortage of cricketers. Everyone will be there watching the final."

"But it's got to be a regular Glory Gardens player. Mack's the only choice."

"Can we have an Aussie playing for us in the World Cup final?" said Cal with a smile.

"I don't see why not. I'll ring him."

Mack was delighted to have another go at beating the West Indians.

"One condition: no parrot," I said.

"Okay, but he'll be terribly disappointed to miss the game."

"Good."

When I came back to the kitchen Cal, Louis and Johnny were watching the Test Match on telly. Things weren't going too well for England. Brian Lara was on 130 and thrashing the bowling all over the ground.

"Another reason why we've got to win," said Cal. "We just can't let the West Indies win everything."

"I'll be shouting for you," said Johnny.

"Oh no," said Lizzie, sticking her fingers in her ears.

———————— ● ————————

We got to the ground early – about an hour before the game was due to start. Kiddo was already there helping Bunter to roll the pitch. So were Azzie, Erica, Jo, Marty and Joe Reddy. There was already quite a big crowd of people having picnics around the boundary.

"Make yourselves useful, kiddoes and put out the boundary rope and markers," shouted Kiddo from the square. Gatting came over and supervised the placing of the markers. If you put one in the wrong place he'd stand by it looking at you with his head on one side until you moved it. When he was satisfied we'd done it properly he wandered back to join Kiddo in the middle.

Soon the Griffiths Hall coach arrived. The bad news was that Thompson Gale was back.

"We've got sausages for tea, Thompson," said Joe. "I know you like them."

Thompson shuddered. "I never want to see another English sausage."

"Anyone seen Frankie?" asked Cal. By now all the others had turned up – even Clive who's nearly always late.

"He was with Joe all morning," said Jo.

"Strange," said Joe. "He got this letter and he sort of wandered off. I haven't seen him since."

I kept the team talk short but I said most of the things Louis and I had talked about the night before. Perhaps it was a good thing Frankie wasn't there, joking and fooling about. Everyone listened to me and there was a kind of determination about them which you don't get every day with Glory Gardens.

I'd almost decided to bat if we won the toss and with Frankie missing, I made my mind up. We could hardly take the field without our wicket-keeper. Unfortunately I lost and Victor decided it for me. "It looks a good track. We'll bat," he said.

Should I tell Azzie to keep wicket until Frankie arrived? I was about to ask him when Joe Reddy said, "Do you want me to put on the gloves? I've brought my kit."

I did wonder for a moment why he'd come along with his cricket gear but I didn't have time to give much thought to it. I asked Victor if it was all right to have a substitute keeper till Frankie arrived and he said it was fine by him.

While Joe got changed we all had a bit of fielding and slip catching practice in front of the pavilion – all except Ohbert who had got his Walkman back and was in a world of his own. Suddenly he let out a cry, "Oh but, it's us on the radio."

"Ohbert's freaked," said Tylan. But at that moment Azzie's dad turned up the radio he was listening to in front of the pavilion. It was Test Match Special and Peter Baxter was talking:

"... *a fine day for the final of the Eastgate Priory World Cup where the home team, Glory Gardens, representing England are playing the West Indies in the form of Griffiths Hall School from Barbados. If you haven't got tickets for Trent Bridge then I suggest you go and watch the English and West Indian under 13s battle it out at the Eastgate Priory ground.*"

We all stood in amazement.

"How did he know about us?" said Tylan.

"Oh but, I think he said someone sent him a cake," said Ohbert.

"My aunt!" said Clive. "I bet it was her."

We all looked at Clive's aunt. She was sitting on the pavilion verandah smiling at us. "Well now we should have a nice big crowd here to watch the match," she chuckled. "I just wish I could make up my mind who to support."

"You don't mean it," said Clive aghast.

"Of course not, only teasing. I may have been born in Barbados but Glory Gardens is my team."

The umpires walked out to the middle and we followed. The final had begun.

Chapter Fourteen

A 40 overs game is very different from 20. For a start each bowler has a maximum of eight overs. So the captain has to think much harder about bowling changes. You need to introduce your weaker bowlers at just the right time and also remember to keep someone back for the last overs when the batters are having a slog.

I opened with Marty and Jacky as usual. I told Marty to bowl flat out for three or four overs and I went on the attack. For Victor Eddy Marty bowled to two slips, a gully, a shortish mid-wicket and no mid-off.

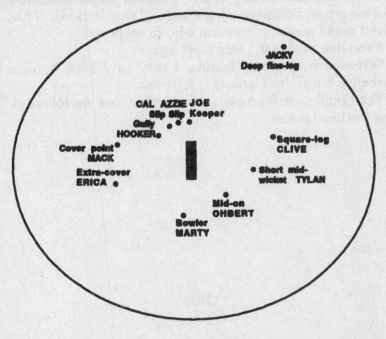

For the other opener, Gary Lomas, who was left-handed, he had a slip, two gullies and a leg slip. I remembered my notes. "Well-pitched-up outside the off-stump to Victor," I said to Marty. "Keep it straight for Gary but drop a couple short." The trap was sprung. Would it work? Marty's first over was a dream. He did everything except take a wicket. Twice he beat Victor outside the off-stump with big away cutters. Then he flicked the top of the batsman's pad and the ball ran away for three leg-byes. Marty appealed but it would have gone well over the stumps. His slower ball then nearly did for Gary who cut it in the air just short of me in the gully. Marty rounded off the over with two more lightning deliveries which the batsman played at and missed.

"What about getting one on the wicket," suggested Joe.

"Just make sure you're ready for the catch," said Marty. "Next over, okay?"

I dropped one of the slips out to square-leg for Jacky and immediately cursed myself when Victor sliced the ball in the air to exactly where second slip would have been. I brought up the slip again and Victor hit the ball through square-leg. He's either lucky or he's good, I thought.

Marty kept up the outside-off-stump assault on Victor. He left two and then played a lovely cover drive. The next ball had Gary on the back foot. It was going down the leg side and he should have left it but, at the last moment, he couldn't resist flicking at it with the bat and got the faintest touch. Joe threw himself across in front of Cal at leg slip and took a brilliant one-handed catch. The ball wouldn't have carried to Cal. And that was the end of Gary Lomas – without scoring.

Henderson Springer announced his arrival with two wild darts at Marty but he didn't even get close to the ball. Victor went down the wicket to have a word with him at the end of the over.

Jacky continued bowling a tight line and length to Victor who had steadied himself with the loss of the wicket. He was now looking to work the ball around the field looking for the

107

gaps. But the fielders were getting to everything: cutting off the fours; turning twos into singles. It was clear that everyone was really fired up. Even Ohbert threw himself full length to stop a straight drive. Unfortunately, he dived over the ball and Jacky had to chase back and retrieve it.

Ohbert picked himself up and brushed down the grass-stained front of his almost-white shirt and trousers. "Oh but . . . I missed," he said.

"Outrageous attempt, Ohbert," said Tylan.

Ohbert squared his puny shoulders and very determinedly walked back to his position. You can never accuse Ohbert of not trying – it's just the results which are a bit peculiar.

"Henderson hooks," I said to Marty as I moved Cal down to the deep backward square-leg trap.

"That's what he thinks," said Marty.

Marty bowled two balls in the block hole, which the batsman just dug out, and then he pitched one short. It got up nicely for Henderson and he hooked it away for two. The next ball was just as short but twice as fast. Henderson went for the hook again. Only at the last minute did he pick up the pace of the ball and then it was on him. It took the top glove and lobbed down the leg side. Joe took off. The ball was going away from him all the time but at the last moment he dived forwards and with arms outstretched took a brilliant catch in both gloves. He rolled over and threw the ball in the air with a howl of triumph. "Caught Reddy, bowled Lear. Again!"

Marty rushed up to congratulate him. "What a team. I'll bowl them; you catch them."

"Not for much longer he won't," said Azzie pointing towards the boundary. There stood the round figure of Frankie, hands on hips beaming all over his face.

"Reddy, steady, go," said Tylan weirdly.

"Where have you been, fatman?" yelled Cal.

"The Wanderer returns," said Joe.

"Get changed," I shouted and Frankie disappeared into the

108

pavilion. Amidst all the excitement I forgot to tell Marty to pitch it up to Cardinal Williams who pulled the second ball he received all along the ground for four in front of square.

After another tight over from Jacky, I told Marty that this was the last one of his spell. He put everything into it. Even Victor was forced to take evasive action to a perfect bouncer which whistled past his chest. We nearly had a run out on the last ball of the over. Cardinal pushed it into the off-side and ran. Victor sent him back and, if Mack's throw had hit, he would have been walking back to the pavilion. Joe reckoned the ball nicked the stumps but didn't dislodge the bail – it was that close.

Frankie swaggered on to the pitch and Joe bowed out. Frankie smacked him over the head with his gloves as they passed.

"So what happened?" asked Cal.

"It's a long story," said Frankie. "And a long walk. I'll tell you later."

"You've got a lot to live up to," said Marty. "He's taken two catches already."

"Two lucky catches and he calls himself a wicket-keeper," said Frankie marking out his position with the studs of his boot.

"We'll settle for you playing half as well," said Cal.

The first byes of the innings came off the second ball of the next over when Frankie let one through his legs. There were groans from all round the field.

I remembered what Louis had said and brought Tylan on to tempt Victor. He opened with his usual wide and then bowled quite well but it was Cardinal and not Victor who faced all seven balls.

After ten overs they had 32 on the board and Victor was looking ominously good on 16. He played another cover-drive off Jacky's next over and then at last he faced Tylan. Tylan pitched up on the off-stump and Victor went for an extravagant drive. The ball shot off the edge between slip and gully for four. Encouraging but expensive.

Suddenly both batsmen were going well. How long could I keep attacking? With the field in close, there was always a chance of taking a wicket but the runs were beginning to flow too fast. I was getting a bit short of ideas. Jacky was still bowling tightly without looking like taking a wicket and Tylan looked like he might take a wicket but he was being punished for his occasional loose ball. Victor hit a full toss for four over mid-on and Cardinal pulled a short delivery to the square-leg boundary. I was forced to defend and for the first time we were on the back foot.

Jacky was just about to begin his last over when Cal walked over. "Have you noticed Cardinal's taking his guard well out of his crease?"

"So what?"

"So if Frankie comes up to the stumps, he'll have to go back behind the crease. He's trying to get on the front foot, so it could unsettle him."

"Do you think Frankie can stand up to Jacky?"

"It might cost us a few byes, but there's only one way to find out."

I told Frankie and he said he was happy to try. Immediately Cardinal took a new guard. The first ball from Jacky was down the leg side and Frankie took it beautifully.

Jacky bowled again. This time Cardinal went forward but he definitely wasn't as confident as before and the ball squirted off a thick outside edge to Clive at point. The third ball of the over was well-pitched-up and the batsman gave it the long handle. He wasn't quite to the pitch of the ball and he got it slightly too high on the bat. The ball was flying over Jacky's head when he shot a hand up and just got his fingers to it. He deflected it to mid-off's left. Erica turned, twisted and dived and took a spectacular one-handed catch almost after the ball had gone past her.

Jacky deserved his wicket. He'd bowled well and he finished his eight-over spell with one for 22. I was considering

The big problem with taking the ball down the leg side is that the batsman blocks your vision and you lose sight of it. Frankie sights the ball on the off-side. Then he moves, leading with his gloves to get in line with the ball. The legs follow side-stepping to the left. Only when he gets across behind the batsman can he see the ball again. Notice he is trying to get his left leg behind the ball as a second line of defence.

a double change because Tylan was proving a bit expensive but with the fall of the wicket I decided to keep him on. He rewarded me with his best over so far. Twice he lured Victor outside the off-stump and twice he played and missed. Then Victor drove him hard into the ground straight to Mack in the covers. Mack caught the ball and threw it high in the air. We all knew it was a bumped ball – but the spectators didn't. A great cheer went up round the ground, followed by a groan when the crowd realised what had happened. Mack grinned.

Erica shows the importance of keeping your eye on the ball all the time. First she has to readjust and dive for the deflection and then she watches the ball all the way into her hand.

I came on to bowl in place of Jacky. I was immediately surprised at the amount of bounce in the pitch. My first ball got up from just short of a length and hit the new batsman, Coventry Phillips on the arm. Frankie claimed the catch behind the wicket but he was the only one to appeal and the Griffiths Hall umpire shook his head.

In my second over I had Victor Eddy dropped, by Azzie of all people, at point. It was a hard low chance to his left and he got both hands to it but it popped out. I looked up at the score-board and saw Victor was on 31. When would we get our next chance I wondered? To add insult to injury he drove my next ball for four through extra-cover – the best shot of the innings.

At the half way stage the West Indies had scored 73 for three. The next ten overs would be vital. A lot was going to depend on how well I bowled. I started thinking about who I was going to bring on at Tylan's end, too. But first Ty had two more overs to bowl. Coventry Phillips went down the wicket to him and Frankie flicked off the bails. Ty punched the air and the batsman began to walk off. The umpire even raised his finger. But none of them noticed that the ball was lying at Frankie's feet. He'd dropped it before he removed the bail. Cal and I called the batsman back.

"Frankie, Frankie," chanted the Durbanville supporters to the right of the pavilion and suddenly they unfurled a long, white banner. It read:

ANOTHER GOLDEN MOMENT FROM FRANKIE

"Joe Reddy's going to suffer for this," said Frankie.

"How do you know it's him?"

"I'd recognise his writing anywhere now. And I bet that's a sheet off my bed."

Frankie made up for his missed stumping in Tylan's last over. I moved Mack slightly deeper in the covers and Coventry hit the ball straight to him and ran. Victor immediately spotted it was Mack and shouted, "No, get back." Coventry turned and slipped and Mack's throw came whistling in to the keeper. But as he stood over the stumps waiting for the ball Frankie knocked a bail off. The throw was perfect and Frankie removed the other bail with the ball just as Coventry was up and running.

"Pull out the stump," yelled Clive.

Frankie didn't hesitate; he grabbed hold of the leg stump and yanked it out of the ground just beating the batsman's sliding, diving attempt to get his bat in. This time the umpire's finger was raised and Coventry was out.

"Why did I have to do that?" asked Frankie.

"Because you knocked the bail off, you fat fool," said Cal. "If a bail is knocked off or blown off, you've got to pull out the stump." He smiled and slapped Frankie on the shoulder. "And you did it beautifully."

Up went the banner again to the cheers of Frankie's 'fan club' and this time Frankie turned and took a bow.

The new batsman didn't last long. I got him with a straight one. He played completely down the wrong line and it knocked out his off-stump. They now had 86 for five and I was quite pleased with the way things were going. My main worry was Victor and when he took 9 off Cal's first over I knew we had to get him out to have a chance of winning. He used his feet well to get to the pitch and just peppered the covers with some brilliant cover drives. Finally when Cal pitched short he stood back and pulled him through mid-wicket to bring up his fifty. It had been a great knock and we all applauded him. But I couldn't help thinking about the chance on 31. I bet Azzie was thinking about it, too.

I bowled a maiden at the new batsman – spoiled only by Frankie letting two byes through his legs. That brought the Frankie Army to their feet again. This time the other side of the banner was displayed – it said:

NICE ONE, FRANKIE

Once again it was Cal versus Victor. Victor struck him for two and then another boundary through the covers.

"I can't afford to keep you on much longer," I said to Cal.

"I know, but I think he's getting over-confident."

"Who can blame him?"

"Can I have another fielder in the covers? You never know – with a bit of luck . . ."

I moved Jacky from square-leg to the gap between cover point and extra-cover and Victor hammered the next ball along the ground straight at him. "Thanks," said Jacky, wringing his hands. "I think I liked it better where I was."

Cal's next ball was given a bit more air and Victor went for the drive again. There was a sharp snick and suddenly I saw it was coming straight at me in the gully. The ball never got above knee high and it was dropping. I fell forwards on my knees and caught it smack in the middle of both hands. Even Victor applauded the catch.

Cal shot a fist in the air in triumph. "The arm ball, the arm ball." He knew just how important that wicket was. We clapped Victor off. He deserved it, he'd scored 57 out of 104 on the board.

"Now let's clean up the tail," said Cal.

With thirteen overs still remaining, I knew that Griffiths Hall could still pile up a very big total but I set a defensive field and for four overs we held them to three an over.

I began my final over. I mixed up the deliveries as much as I could. First a yorker, then a slow off-break and then a quicker one fired into the pads. The first four were dot balls and the batsman was showing signs of frustration. He took a wild swing at the fifth which was another slow delivery and it went straight up off a top edge. It was going over my head. But if I ran back, I could probably get it.

"Jacky," shouted Cal.

Jacky was at mid-on. Yes, it was his catch. I stopped running. Jacky moved to his left. He was under the ball. It hit his hands, bounced up and he grasped it to his chest on the second attempt.

"Whew," he said. "Thought I'd lost it." It was a good catch. No-one likes taking the high ones; you have too long to think about it and it's always a relief when you've got the ball in your hands.

At the end of my over I immediately took Cal off and brought Marty back to polish off the tail enders. It didn't quite work out like that. Thompson Gale cracked two fours off him.

I brought on Erica at my end and she was smacked for four, too. This was getting dangerous. Thompson isn't the most delicate of batsmen but he can definitely hit a cricket ball.

The faster Marty bowled the harder Thompson clouted him. I posted a long-on and deep mid-wicket to cover his favourite shots but then Marty dropped one short and he hooked it savagely over square-leg for another four.

With five overs left I could hardly wait for the innings to end. If Thompson carried on like this we'd have a mountain to climb. Erica's next over went for only four runs, which seemed brilliant after what had just been happening. And then Marty resumed his battle with Thompson.

I don't think Marty had ever bowled to a more defensive field.

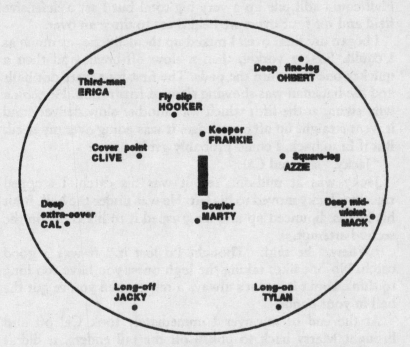

Deep fine-leg
OHBERT

Third-man
ERICA

Fly slip
HOOKER

Keeper
FRANKIE

Cover point
CLIVE

Square-leg
AZZIE

Deep
extra-cover
CAL

Bowler
MARTY

Deep mid-
wicket
MACK

Long-off
JACKY

Long-on
TYLAN

Only Azzie, Clive and I were up saving the one; the rest of the field were all posted out on the boundary. Ohbert let one through his legs for four and then Tylan dropped a skier running in from long-on. I switched him with Clive, who was at cover point – Clive's a better catcher than Ty. If I'd thought of that earlier Thompson would now be back in the pavilion. Eight more came off the over.

Erica tightened it up again with yet another mean over which cost only four runs. 150 came up on the board and there were still two overs to bowl. Marty began his last over. He stopped a searing straight drive from Thompson with his right hand. It must have hurt because the ball seemed to be travelling at 100 miles an hour, but Marty didn't show it. He bowled a fast yorker which hit Thompson on the toe and had him hopping about. Then he produced a beauty which nearly cut Thompson in two; it darted in between bat and pad and knocked out his middle stump. Thompson had scored 33 out of 36 which had come at a run a ball.

Erica's last over was on the spot again and Griffiths Hall finished on 160.

"Exactly four an over," said Cal. "We can do it."

"They shouldn't have got that many," said Marty. "It's my fault."

"Cheer up, Mart," said Frankie. "When you bat like Thompson or me, even the best bowlers get carted all over the park."

INNINGS OF: GRIFFITHS HALL   TOSS WON BY: G.H.   WEATHER: SUNNY

BATSMAN	RUNS SCORED	HOW OUT	BOWLER	SCORE
1 V. EDDY	2·2·1·3·2·1·1·2·2·2·4·1·1·6·1· 1·(3)·4·2·1·2·1·2·2·2·3·(2)·4·4	ct KNIGHT	SEBASTIEN	57
2 G. LOMAS		ct SUB	LEAR	0
3 H. SPRINGER	2	ct SUB	LEAR	2
4 C. WILLIAMS	4·1·1·1·2·2·4·1	ct DAVIES	GUNN	16
5 C. PHILLIPS	1·1·1·2·1·3	RUN	OUT	9
6 V. TOSSELL		bowled	KNIGHT	0
7 W. HAYNES	1·0·1·2·1·	ct GUNN	KNIGHT	6
8 T. GALE	2·1·4·4·1·4·4·2·1·4·3·2·1	bowled	LEAR	33
9 C. CUMBERLAND	1·1·1·2·1·	NOT	OUT	7
10 R. KING	2·1·1	NOT	OUT	4
11				

FALL OF WICKETS										BYES	2·1·1·2·2·2		10	TOTAL EXTRAS	26
SCORE	11	15	59	81	84	104	114	150			LEG BYES	3·1·1·1·1·2·3·1·1		13	TOTAL	160
BAT NO	2	3	4	5	6	7	8				WIDES	1·1·1		3	FOR	
										NO BALLS				WKTS	8

SCORE AT A GLANCE

BOWLER	1	2	3	4	5	6	7	8	9	10	11	12	13	OVS	MDS	RUNS	WKT
1 M. LEAR	M	·3· W·	·2· ···	X	··4· ·4·1	·4· ·4·3	W· ·1·	2·1						8	1	35	3
2 J. GUNN	·2· 2·1	2· ···	2· ·1·	1· ···	··· 2·2	·2· ·1·	1· ·1·	X						8	0	22	1
3 T. VELLACOTT	1··· ·1··	1··· ····	··4· ·1··	1··· ·1··	··· ·1··	··4· ·1··	·11· ·1··	X						8	0	29	0
4 H. KNIGHT	···· ·1··	4··· ··1·	·2·1 ·W·1	M	·1· ·2·2	W	X							8	2	17	2
5 C. SEBASTIEN	2·1 ·4·	··· ·1·	··· ··1	X										4	0	18	1
6 E. DAVIES	··· ·1·	·1· ·2·1	··2·1 ·1·1	··· ·11										4	0	16	0
7																	
8																	
9																	

Chapter Fifteen

"Why were you late, Francis?" demanded Jo. "Because of this," said Frankie. It was a letter typed on printed writing paper with Kiddo's address at the top.

> Dear Francis,
> Sorry this is very late notice but the game today has been transferred to the Wyckham Wanderers ground. I'll explain why when you get there.
> See you at 1.30 sharp.
> Yours
>
> *P. Johnstone*
>
> P. Johnstone

"Even the signature looks like Kiddo's," said Frankie.

"And you fell for it," said Cal. "Some people are born suckers."

"But who did it?" asked Azzie.

"If I were a betting person, which of course I'm not," said Frankie, "I'd put all my money on . . ."

"Joe," said Cal.

"I wonder how he got hold of Kiddo's writing paper," I said.

"There's plenty in the club room in the pavilion," said Jo.

"But it's not that far to the Wyckham ground. What took you so long?"

"I was late. I didn't get there till ten to two."

"Typical! I knew I shouldn't have let you out of my sight," sighed Jo.

"Never mind," said Frankie. "I've put a kipper in his suitcase. It should be nice and ripe by the time he arrives in South Africa."

"You can't do that," said Jo. "He'll get arrested for bringing food into the country – it's illegal."

"Good," said Frankie.

"Well I'm going to tell him," said Jo.

"Typical," sighed Frankie.

The Durbanville team were walking up and down in front of the pavilion with the 'Frankie' banner. "10 byes, 10 byes," chanted Joe. "There he is, fans. The late, great Frankie Allen." And all the Durbanville players cheered.

By now the crowd was enormous. There must have been nearly two hundred people watching the game.

"Best turn out we've ever had, kiddoes." Kiddo was enjoying himself. He loves telling people that Glory Gardens is 'his team' and how much the 'little lads' have come on this year. It makes you want to throw up sometimes but I suppose it keeps him happy. Mack's whole family was there, minus the parrot, and quite a lot of the Azdadz, the Acks and the Wanderers had come along, too. Gatting was scavenging from people's picnics around the boundary.

"Who's opening?" Azzie asked me. I showed him the batting order.

C. Sebastien	F. Allen
H. Knight	T. Vellacott
A. Nazar	M. Lear
C. da Costa	J. Gun
E. Davies	P. Bennett
T. McCurdy	

I'd decided to open the innings for a change, partly to see if it would bring my run of low scores to an end, but also, with Mack and Frankie at six and seven, I needed Erica in the middle order to steady things down. And anyway, I fancied opening for once, although I wasn't sure I was looking forward to Thompson Gale and Richard Wallace.

"Don't panic if you fall behind the clock, kiddo," said Kiddo. "It's wickets that count in these games. Just stay there and the runs will come."

Cal and I walked out to a tremendous round of applause.

"You face first," I said. "And watch out for the yorker."

"Who's the senior opener?" said Cal with a grin. "Don't try anything fancy and remember – quick singles, but don't run me out."

"Best of luck," I said.

Richard Wallace's first ball flew over the stumps and I'm not sure Cal saw it. It was lightning fast. I started doing some stretching exercises to help me concentrate. The next one shot off an inside edge for a single and suddenly I was facing the quickest Under 13s bowler I'd ever seen.

Get forward – I told myself. I did and met the ball in the middle of the bat. That felt better. The next two passed harmlessly outside the off-stump and I was beginning to get the pace of the pitch. Richard finished the over with a toe-crushing yorker. I clamped the bat down on it and the ball ran wide of square-leg for a single. I was off the mark!

Thompson was perhaps a little slower than Richard, but at this pace it didn't make much difference. He was bowling wide of the crease and firing the ball into me. I clipped a short one off my hip for two. Then he got one to hold up a little off the pitch and it went past the outside edge of my groping bat.

Get your foot across – I said to myself, practising the shot I should have played. Cal was dropped in the slips next over. Two balls later Richard knocked out his off-stump with a perfect length delivery. The stump did a cartwheel and Richard punched the air.

121

"They're both quick," I said to Azzie as if that wasn't obvious. "Play yourself in." But I knew Azzie would play the only way he knows, taking the attack to the bowlers. He got a short one from Thompson which hit him on the shoulder and then he cover drove the next for three. Thompson was now bowling wide of the off-stump to tempt me to edge to the slips. He pushed one a bit too far out and he was called for a wide.

Azzie and I met in the middle again. "I think they're both getting over-excited," said Azzie. "They're bowling more with their arms than their brains."

"All I know is their arms are fast. Are you picking the ball up okay?" I asked.

"Now and again," grinned Azzie.

I'd decided to play the anchor-role. I ran a single down to third-man off Richard Wallace and then Azzie hooked him in the air for four. Richard didn't like that and his next ball was fast and nearly cut Azzie in two. It passed just over the stumps.

With a few near misses and some brilliant shots Azzie got into double figures. Then he chased a wide delivery from Thompson Gale. If he'd left it, it would have probably been called a wide. He got a nick to the keeper and walked without waiting for the umpire's decision.

We were 27 for two after eight overs and both the quickies came off. I wasn't sorry. Victor brought Cardinal Williams on at the canal end and after one over I realised he was one of the West Indies' weaker bowlers. Victor was probably trying to use up a few of his overs while we were on the defensive. Not that Cardinal was bad; he pitched the ball just short of a length, bowling medium-pace seamers and it wasn't easy to get him away. But I knew I had to cash in on Cardinal's bowling if I could, so that we didn't put ourselves under too much pressure later on.

Victor Eddy, who came on at the other end, was a different matter. He bowled mean little off-cutters, on a length all the time. He was too quick to go down the track to, so most of the time all I could do was play him defensively off the front foot or try to work him away on the leg side where he'd got three fielders stopping the single.

Fortunately, Clive took over where Azzie had left off. He began to dominate the bowling in the way he does best. First he pushed them on the defensive with a couple of hits over the in-field. Then, when they'd got fielders back on the boundary, he cashed in with singles and twos into the spaces.

Extra-cover is back on the boundary. Clive gently pushes the ball in his direction and we run two. If he'd hit it hard, it would have reached the fielder more quickly and we'd have got only a single.

Ten came off Cardinal's third over and Victor immediately took him off and replaced him with his spinner, Vaughan Tossell. I tried to remember what Louis had said about Vaughan. Sharp leg spin and lots of bounce – I think.

His first ball was a full toss and I whacked it away for three. The next took Clive completely by surprise. It pitched on leg stump and he pushed forward down the line. It turned and lifted and took the glove on the way through to Henderson behind the stumps. He caught it at the second attempt. 55 for three.

It was a good moment for Erica to come in. We needed to consolidate. If another couple of wickets fell now we'd be in real trouble.

"Jo says we're well up with the clock – they had 49 after 13 overs," Erica said.

"No hurry then," I said. "Play your normal game and watch out for the leggie. He turns it."

It got harder and harder to score. Victor was sealing one end and that meant we either had to take our chances against Vaughan or wait for a bowling change.

Just ten runs came off the next five overs. The twentieth over was bowled and our score had limped up to 68. I heard a loud yawn from Frankie and sensed the Glory Gardens supporters were beginning to get restless. I did a quick calculation. It wasn't too bad – we now needed about 4½ an over. No need to go mad but it was time to accelerate a little.

In the next over I went down the pitch to the spinner and hit him over the top for three. Then Erica took a single and I drove him for another two.

Frankie and Cal came on with drinks at the end of the over.

"We thought we'd bring these out to wake you up," said Frankie.

"Shouldn't you be padded up?" Erica asked Frankie.

"No need. You look as if you're going to bat all week."

"How are we doing?" I asked Cal.

"Fine. A bit behind the clock but nothing to panic about. Perhaps you could push a few more singles. We don't want to be under too much pressure against the quickies at the end."

Erica took a fresh guard after the break, just to get her concentration going again. She played out a maiden from Victor – every ball was on the spot. I looked round the field before I faced up to the spinner again. There weren't too many gaps. Up to me to create a few then. I swung one away in the air behind square for four and then realised with a bit of a shock that it was the first boundary of my innings. Victor immediately dropped Thompson back to deep square-leg.

A couple of balls later the spinner fed me a short one and I fell for it. I went for another leg side swing but as I played it I knew the ball was going in the air. Thompson was waiting out on the square-leg boundary. It was a high swirling catch and for a second I stood and watched in despair. "Run!" shouted Erica and I ran like the wind. I couldn't believe my luck when I looked again – there was Thompson picking the ball up off the ground. He'd dropped it.

"Hard luck, Tommo," shouted Victor. He was clapping his hands to motivate the fielders and shouting encouragement every time someone stopped a run or threw in over the stumps. But he never once got on a player's back when he made a mistake.

I began to calculate the number of overs left. 17, I reckoned. Eight more from the quickies, three from Vaughan, one from Victor. That meant someone else had to bowl at least four overs. Who would it be? Would Victor bring back Cardinal Williams or go for a completely fresh bowler? I watched him preparing to bowl his last over. Suddenly he hesitated and decided on a bowling change. On came his sixth bowler. This was the moment I'd been waiting for. The new bowler wasn't bad, but he was a friendly pace and I cracked him for two twos on the off. He pitched short and I pulled him for four down to backward square-leg.

Vaughan Tossell was still bowling brilliantly at the other end and at last he managed to lure Erica down the track. She didn't get to the pitch and she missed the ball completely and was smartly stumped by Henderson, the keeper. Though she'd only scored 5, she'd held up an end for ten overs while I pushed the score along. It had been a vital innings and as soon as she was out the West Indies were back on top again.

Mack joined me with the score on 88 for four. He was

immediately beaten twice by the spinner; then he swept wildly and got it very fine for four.

Although he played the medium-pacer well, Mack continued to have a terrible time against Vaughan. He kept flailing away and missing. But slowly the score crept through the nineties and finally I brought up the hundred with a little off-side nudge. The very next ball, Mack tried to lift one over long-off and succeeded only in spooning a catch straight back to Vaughan.

Frankie came to the wicket to enormous cheers from his 'fan club'. The banner was waved; first one side, then the other. There was a great chant of "Frankie, Frankie" – you could hear Johnny Malan's voice loud and clear over all the others. Everyone within twenty yards of him must have been deafened.

"I've got a few messages for you," said Frankie as he reached the middle. "First, Jo says that they had 108 after the same number of overs – so we're not far behind. Second, we need about five an over and . . . I can't remember the last thing she told me."

"Well I've got a message for you," I said. "Vaughan's only got three balls left. So get down the track to him and just get something in the way. Bat, pads, anything. Only don't try to hit him out of the ground."

"Aye, aye, captain."

It didn't look pretty but Frankie for once did just as he was told. Three times he walked down the wicket and kicked the ball away. The last time Vaughan had a huge shout for lbw, but Frankie was so far down the track that there was no way Sid was going to give it.

I hit a juicy half-volley for three off the second ball of the next over. After we'd run them Frankie came panting down the wicket towards me.

"I've just remembered what it was," he gasped.

"What?"

"You were on 46 – so that must make it 49."

Chapter Sixteen

The last thing I wanted to know was that I needed one for my fifty. It would be my first for Glory Gardens (I'd scored 62 once for the Colts). I was so jumpy I nearly ran myself out next ball calling Frankie for a quick leg bye that was never there. I'd have been out by a mile if the fielder hadn't made a mess of his throw, but at least it gave me the strike again. Concentrate! I said to myself. I played two careful forward defensive strokes. Then I got one pitched-up on the leg stump and I gave it the full on drive treatment. From the moment it left the bat I knew it was four runs. I took a couple of steps down the wicket and raised my bat to the cheers of the crowd. Frankie rushed down the pitch and tried to lift me up. A couple of the West Indians came and shook my hand.

I looked up at the score-board. There was my 53 – next to the total – 108 for five. But there was no relaxing now; we still had to win the match and there was a long way to go.

As I expected, Victor turned to pace again. Richard Wallace came on from the top end as before and his second ball of the spell was a vicious yorker which landed straight on Frankie's toe. He rolled over on his back holding his left foot.

NICE ONE, FRANKIE – up went the banner again and the Frankie Army started chanting the words, too. Frankie pulled his boot off and stared at his swelling big toe which stuck out of the end off his sawn-off sock. The West Indian stared at his toes in amazement.

My dream on drive. The ball is over-pitched on leg stump and I place my left leg outside the line of the ball – that makes sure your head's over it and you're well balanced – and the bat moves cleanly in an arc from slips to mid-on. Notice how the weight of the body is transferred on to the front foot.

"Do you want to go off?" I asked.

"No, I'll carry on," said Frankie pulling himself to his feet and hobbling on the injured foot. He put the boot back on and hobbled a little more. "I think I might need a runner, though."

Oh no, I thought. A runner is nearly always a recipe for disaster, but if Frankie's involved it's a dead cert. Mack had only taken one of his pads off since he was out, so he buckled it on again and came out to run for Frankie. The rest of Richard's over was devastating. He certainly didn't show any mercy for Frankie's toe. Every ball was in the block hole and

Frankie danced and jumped to keep his toe out of the way. He was clean bowled off a no ball and very close to lbw; but somehow he survived the over.

At the other end I hit a four over point with an uppish cut and then I pushed a quick single on the off-side. Forgetting he had a runner Frankie started to run and then fell over wincing with the pain. Mack was watching him and set off late and there was a moment when I thought he wasn't going to make it but he grounded his bat just in time. I picked Frankie up.

"I think you'd better stay down that end for a bit and keep away from Richard." I said. "Tell Mack not to run for any singles this over."

So I faced Richard Wallace again. The first ball was fast but it was a no ball. The light wasn't as good as it had been earlier and although I was seeing the ball well, it wasn't pleasant for a new batsman coming in. All the more reason to stay there. A wide and another no ball gave me a bit of respite. Then Richard bowled again. Frankie was watching him run in from square-leg, Mack was looking at the bowling crease, too. As Richard bowled they both looked at each other and signalled 'no ball' to each other. But the umpire didn't. The ball hit my pad and ran down the leg side. I waited for the call but Mack wasn't looking. Frankie looked up and started to run. I took off. Mack hadn't moved. I stopped and turned to see the fielder swooping on the ball. With a full length dive I just got my bat back in in time.

"What's going on?" I said as I walked over to Mack.

"But his foot was miles over the line . . ." he began.

"It was," insisted Frankie.

"You're out here to run, not umpire," I said to Mack.

"I thought you said no singles," said Mack with a grin.

I had to admit I'd forgotten about that. "Well er . . . I'll try and get a single off the last ball."

I played the rest of the over defensively and then nudged the sixth ball down to fine-leg to keep the strike. Back came Thompson Gale at the other end. The light was definitely getting worse and I reckoned with seven overs to go we now needed nearly six an over. I hammered a four with a slashing cut drive which split the covers and then got a thick edge for two. I tried to keep the strike off the last ball but it went straight to a fielder. That left Frankie to face Richard's toe crushers again. He top-edged a short one over the keeper's head for four and then he got another yorker which he tried to drive. The ball took an edge on to his pad and trickled back towards the stumps.

"Look out," shouted Mack. Frankie turned and saw the ball about to roll into the stumps. For some weird reason, instead of kicking it away he put his hand on the bails and held them in position. The ball hit the stumps but, of course, the bails didn't fall. Frankie took his glove away and grinned at the umpire. The bails were still there.

The umpire hesitated then raised his finger.

"But the bails didn't fall off," protested Frankie.

The two umpires conferred and finally sent Frankie and Mack on their way. "I still don't see how I'm out. You're not out if the bails don't fall off." said Frankie to Mack. The Durbanville band burst into another crescendo as Frankie limped up the pavilion steps waving to them.

129 for six. We needed to score 32 off the West Indian pace attack with only Ty and Marty, Jacky and Ohbert to come. Ty got behind the first one and edged the second just wide of the keeper for a single. I wanted a single or a three to keep the strike but I got one short and wide of the off-stump and cut it away crisply for four.

Tylan completely missed his first three balls from Thompson – in the growing gloom he probably couldn't see them at all. Then a top edge for two and a leg bye gave him the strike again for the next over.

"It's 24 from four overs – a run a ball," I said to Tylan. "Push it in front of you and we run, okay?"

"I will if I see it," said Tylan.

Ty aimed a wild swing at the first and missed but it went

through for two byes. He jammed the bat down on the second and ran. I knew immediately I was out. He'd got too much bat on it and the ball sped straight to the one close fielder on the leg side. Although I was backing up, I knew I wouldn't have a chance if his throw was good. It was. I was run out by several feet. I'd scored 69 – and I was furious, more with myself than with Tylan. We've thrown it away, I thought, just when it was there for the winning. You could see that the West Indians thought they had it in the bag now, too. They were jumping around like Mack's puppies.

Marty looked very determined as he walked out. He didn't say a word to me as we passed; he just stared straight ahead, his eyes fixed on the wicket. He took guard and peered towards the receding figure of Richard Wallace. Richard welcomed him with a fast, shortish ball but Marty got well on top of it and played it down with a very straight bat. He then ran two from a yorker that deflected off his boot. Richard finished with a maiden but four had come in extras. There were three overs left now; two to Thompson and I guessed Victor would bowl the other. We needed 20 to win.

"We've got to go for Victor," I said, wishing I was still out there.

"Don't worry, Marty and Ty can handle themselves," said Cal without sounding too confident.

"They had 146 after 37 overs," said Jo. "We're only five behind."

Jo's chart shows the scores for both teams at the end of every over. You can see how close it is.

	1	2	3	4	5	6	7	8	9	10	11	12	13	14	15	16
Griffiths Hall	3	8	11	13	19	22	24	28	32	35	40	44	49	52	58	59
Glory Gardens	2	5	8	13	18	21	25	27	30	32	37	41	51	52	55	56

	17	18	19	20	21	22	23	24	25	26	27	28	29	30
Griffiths Hall	61	64	69	73	76	80	81	85	94	96	102	105	108	112
Glory Gardens	58	61	64	68	75	75	80	88	92	96	98	99	100	108

	31	32	33	34	35	36	37	38	39	40
Griffiths Hall	114	114	123	129	134	138	146	150	154	160
Glory Gardens	110	115	119	125	134	137	141			

Tylan squirted two twos off Thompson who was bowling a bit too short, trying to get extra bounce out of the pitch. If this light wasn't good for the batsmen it wasn't helping the fielders either. One of them ran the wrong way when the ball was coming towards him. Then Thompson bowled a no ball to give us five off the over. That left 15 to win off two.

"Go for it, Marty," I whispered under my breath.

Victor Eddy bowled his last over from the Woodcock Lane end. Marty hit his second ball hard and high over square-leg for four to bring up the 150. The cheers rang round the ground. But the ball was lost in the thick hedge on the far side of the ground. They spent five minutes looking for it and then old Sid produced a new ball. There was another delay while Victor rearranged his field. The light was getting worse and worse.

At last Victor resumed his over. He kept his nerve and bowled on the spot. Tylan and Marty managed only three more singles off it.

"Eight to win," said Jo in a tense voice.

Now the crowd was really buzzing. The last over began. Marty pushed a single off the first ball. Then Thompson bowled a slower one to Tylan who didn't pick it up and spooned an easy catch to mid-on.

"Go for it," Cal said to Jacky as he got up from his seat.

Seven off four balls – it wasn't possible, was it?

I don't think Jacky saw his first ball from Thompson. It hit his pads and Marty was down the pitch for the run before the fielders could move. The fourth ball of the over was short and Marty hooked it off his nose. It was stopped on the boundary but they still ran two. 157 – four to win.

Marty swung hard at the next. It was wide of the off-stump. He missed. A groan went round the ground. Then slowly the umpire raised his arms and signalled a wide. We cheered. Still two balls to go. Three runs to win.

Marty looked around the field. There weren't many gaps where he could score two. Thompson raced in and bowled. It was just short of a length outside the off-stump. Marty watched it and at the last moment played the most delicate of late cuts. "Two," he shouted and Jacky ran. He ran so fast that he had completed his two runs well before Marty. But Marty ran his bat in at the danger end to beat the throw.

Marty plays the late cut very fine to avoid the fielders. The ball has almost passed the stumps when he plays it down with a last second flick of the wrists.

The scores were level. Victor brought everyone up on the single. There was a murmuring from the crowd as Thompson walked back slowly to his mark. And then silence. He started to run in. As he reached the crease I wanted to close my eyes. The ball was straight, on middle stump. Marty just managed to get his bat on it and he ran. Jacky was backing up so far that he was through for the single almost before Marty took off. The short mid-wicket fielder picked up and hurled the ball at the bowler's end. For a horrible moment I thought it was going to hit the stumps, but it flashed by. Thompson, positioned just behind the stumps, took it cleanly and knocked off the bails. But in that split second, Marty's bat was home. We'd won!

Marty carried on running all the way to the pavilion, his bat raised high. The crowd was on its feet cheering.

While Frankie danced round the ground singing "Glory, Glory Hallelujah" I walked out to shake hands with Victor and the West Indians. They got an enormous round of applause from the crowd as they came in. Victor was about as happy as I'd have been to have lost by one run. "We should have beaten you," he said. "But you deserved it. You took your chances. A great game."

Frankie appeared draped in his banner; he was still limping but it didn't seem to worry him. "You'll tell them all about Glory Gardens when you get back to Barbados, won't you, Thompson?"

"What do you want me to do? Sing a calypso?" asked Thompson with a smile.

Frankie thought for a moment and then he sang:

The World Cup favourites are Griffiths Hall,
And one by one they beat them all.
But in the final they ran out of steam,
And lost to Glory Gardens Cricket Team.
Yes, the great Glory Gardens Cricket Team.

Frankie bowed and everyone laughed. So, of course, he sang it again and again.

The 'World Cup' turned out to be an enormous cake in the shape of a trophy. Clive's aunt had made it and on its side were the words UNDER 13s WORLD CUP. She was still busy putting the last touches to it – adding underneath, WINNERS: GLORY GARDENS C.C.

The World Cup had come to an end and we were the champions. It was a moment to relish. Griffiths Hall were the best team we'd ever faced and we'd beaten them – not because we were better players than them but because we'd all played as a team. That was the great thing. Glory Gardens hasn't always played with team spirit; in fact, there've been times when I've despaired of them all – like the big row over selecting Ohbert and Clive's arrogant behaviour which nearly forced Jacky to leave the team. But right through the World Cup every single player had batted and bowled and fielded like demons for Glory Gardens.

It had been a brilliant two weeks. I remembered Mack's amazing innings against the West Indians, Matt's batting and Jacky's bowling against the Azdadz. I thought of Cal's 49 in the first game with Durbanville and, of course, my 69 today in the final. And I'd never forget the Griffiths Hall pace twins, Thompson and Richard, and Victor Eddy's batting.

Joe and Frankie brought their war to a peaceful truce – and when Jo told Joe about the secret weapon kipper in his case, Joe laughed his head off.

"It just won't be the same when you've gone, Joe," said Frankie. "Everyone around here is too sensible."

"What a shame they're not all as mad as us," said Joe laughing.

Everyone seemed happy that evening. Even Brad Miller was smiling, probably because his ordeal with Ohbert and his family was over at last. Ohbert had somehow got hold of a load of his little lucky plastic green frogs and he was handing them out to everyone in sight. Frankie refused to take one. "The last person to take one of these got chicken pox," he said. "I think they're plague frogs."

Poor old Matthew, I thought. He'd be so sick to be missing the final, but he'd played his part in getting us here.

Finally it was time for the presentation. Kiddo stood on the pavilion steps next to the magnificent cake. He said a few yukky things about the teams and the 'truly exceptional competition' and then he said, "I've asked an old friend of mine to make the presentations today. And here he is."

From behind him in the doorway of the pavilion a voice was heard to say, "Thank you, Prof and good evening everyone. What an absolutely fabulous finish. And my word it's very good to be here."

"Joe?" said Frankie.

"Frankie?" said Joe. They stared at each other with open mouths and then at the figure standing next to Kiddo.

"It can't be," said Frankie.

"I don't believe it," said Joe.

"It's RICHIE BENAUD!" they both gasped.

Standing on the steps of the Priory pavilion was the real Richie Benaud. "I'd like to present this magnificent trophy to the winning captain and – there's no doubt about it in my mind – the Man of the Match, Harry Knight," he said. A great cheer went up and Frankie and Joe chanted, "Hooker, Hooker," as I went up to receive the cake. Richie Benaud shook my hand and he said he wished he'd been here for the whole game because it sounded a lot more thrilling than the Test Match. I was so excited I nearly dropped the cake.

"I bet he's come because he heard us on the radio," said Joe.

"My word, I can't wait to talk to him," said Frankie.

"Shut up, Francis," hissed Jo.

"I'm going to ask him if I was really out," said Frankie. "He'll know if there's a law against holding the bails on."

Richie Benaud also handed out medals to everyone who had played in the final and there were pennants for all the teams who had taken part in the World Cup.

Frankie went up to get our pennant and he told Richie Benaud that he was his greatest fan. "So you must be Frankie," said Richie Benaud with a smile. "The Prof tells me you're a radio star. You must give me a few tips sometime."

Frankie went bright red.

We ate the cake. Clive's aunt insisted on saving a bit for

Matthew but the rest of it disappeared in seconds, which wasn't surprising because it was delicious.

Then the Durbanville coach arrived and it was time for them all to go.

"See you in South Africa," shouted Louis out of the window.

"Definitely. One day." I said.

"Why not get on the coach and come with us now?" suggested Joe.

The last sounds we heard were from Johnny Malan as the coach disappeared down the Priory Road. Soon the crowd began to leave. The Acks and the Azdadz and Griffiths Hall all said goodbye. And soon the Priory ground was almost empty – the only noise came from the pavilion bar which was busier than usual for a Saturday night.

Cal and I sat on the pavilion steps. The sound of Gatting snoring rose up from his den below.

"Glory Garden World Champions! It's like a dream, Hooker," said Cal.

"Yeah," I said. "Where do we go from here?"

INNINGS OF GLORY GARDENS ...... TOSS WON BY G.H. WEATHER Cloudy

BATSMAN	RUNS SCORED	HOW OUT	BOWLER	SCORE
1 C. SEBASTIEN	1.2	bowled	WALLACE	3
2 H. KNIGHT	1.2.1.1.1.1.3.1.1.1.1.3.1.1.2.2.1.3.2.4 / 3.3.1.3.(4)(4)1.1.1.1.3.4.4.1.1.4.2.4 /	RUN	OUT	69
3 A. NAZAR	3.4.1.2.1.2	ct SPRINGER	GALE	13
4 C. DA COSTA	1.3.1.2.2.4	ct SPRINGER	TOSSELL	13
5 E. DAVIES	1.1.1.1.1	st SPRINGER	TOSSELL	5
6 T. McCURDY	4.2.1.1	C X D	TOSSELL	8
7 F. ALLEN	4	bowled	WALLACE	4
8 T. VELLACOTT	1.2.2.2.1	ct HAYNES	GALE	8
9 M. LEAR	4.1.1.1.2.2.1	NOT	OUT	12
10 J. GUNN		NOT	OUT	0
11 P. BENNETT				

FALL OF WICKETS											BYES	2.2		4	TOTAL EXTRAS	26
SCORE	7	27	65	88	100	129	139	124			LEG BYES	1.1.1.1.1.1.1.1.2.1		11	TOTAL FOR	161
BAT NO	1	3	4	5	6	7	2	8			WIDES	1.1.1.1.1.1		6		
											NO BALLS	1.1.1.1		5	WKTS	8

SCORE AT A GLANCE

BOWLER	1	2	3	4	5	6	7	8	9	10	11	12	13	OVS	MDS	RUNS	WKT
1 R. WALLACE					X			M	X					8	1	28	2
2 T. GALE					X									8	0	32	2
3 C. WILLIAMS				X										3	0	17	0
4 V. EDDY			M				M		X					8	2	19	0
5 V. TOSSELL								X						8	0	25	3
6 R. KING					X									5	0	25	0
7																	
8																	
9																	

BOWLING ANALYSIS ⊙ NO BALL + WIDE

GLORY GARDENS World Cup Averages

Batting

	Inns	Not out	Runs	S/R	H/S	Average
Matthew	3	1	40	31.2	39*	20.0
Hooker	4	0	77	73.4	69	19.3
Cal	4	0	63	55.8	49	15.8
Clive	4	0	47	89.1	24	11.8
Azzie	4	0	44	96.0	19	11.0
Erica	4	1	33	42.3	16*	11.0

* denotes 'not out'. Scoring (S/R) is based on the average number of runs scored per 100 balls. H/S = highest score. Minimum qualification: 30 runs.

Bowling

	Overs	Mdns	Runs	Wkts	S/R	Econ	Average
Hooker	15.4	2	43	5	18.8	2.7	8.6
Marty	19	1	76	7	16.2	4.0	10.9
Jacky	20	0	60	5	24.0	3.0	12.0
Cal	15	2	49	4	22.5	3.3	12.3
Erica	12	0	40	3	24.0	3.3	13.3
Tylan	18	0	81	5	21.6	4.5	16.2

Strike rate (S/R) is the average number of balls bowled to take each wicket. Economy rate (ECON) is the average number of runs given away each over. Minimum qualification: 3 wickets.

Catches

	Caught	Dropped	Total
Hooker	3	0	+3
Azzie	3	1	+2
Frankie	3	1	+2
Cal	1	0	+1
Erica	1	0	+1
Jacky	1	1	0
Marty	1	1	0
Matthew	0	1	-1
Ohbert	0	2	-2
Tylan	0	2	-2

World Cup Ratings

Batsmen – leading run scorers

	No of Inns	Total Runs
Victor Eddy, Griffiths Hall	4	167
Hooker Knight, Glory Gardens	4	77
Yousef Mohamed, Mr Nazar's XI	3	71
Carlton Williams, Griffiths Hall	4	70
R Mattis, Mack's Academy	3	68

Bowlers – leading wicket takers

	No of Games	Total Wickets
Richard Wallace, Griffiths Hall	4	14
Kiran Bharatkumar, Mr Nazar's XI	3	10
Vaughan Tossell, Griffiths Hall	4	9
Kipper Hawkes, Mack's Academy	3	7
Marty Lear, Glory Gardens	4	7

Top Wicket-keepers

	No of Games	Caught	Stumped	Total
Sam Keeping, Mack's Academy	3	5	2	7
Henderson Springer, Griffiths Hall	4	4	2	6
Frankie Allen, Glory Gardens	4	3	2	5
Joe Reddy, Durbanville	3*	4	1	5

*Joe Reddy played as sub for Glory Gardens in the final and his two catches in this game are included here.

THE CRICKET PITCH

crease   At each end of the wicket the crease is marked out in white paint like this:

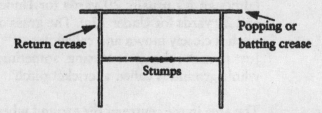

The batsman is 'in his ground' when his bat or either foot are behind the batting or 'popping' crease. He can only be given out 'stumped' or 'run out' if he is outside the crease.

The bowler must not put his front foot down beyond the popping crease when he bowls. And his back foot must be inside the return crease. If he breaks these rules the umpire will call a 'no ball'.

leg side/
off-side   The cricket pitch is divided down the middle. Everything on the side of the batsman's legs is called the 'leg side' or 'on side' and the other side is called the 'off-side'.

Remember, when a left-handed bat is batting, his legs are on the other side. So leg side and off-side switch round.

leg stump   Three stumps and two bails make up each wicket. The 'leg stump' is on the same side as the batsman's legs. Next to it is the 'middle stump' and then the 'off-stump'.

off/on side	See **leg side**
off-stump	See **leg stump**
pitch	The 'pitch' is the area between the two wickets. It is 22 yards long from wicket to wicket (although it's usually 20 yards for Under 11s and 21 yards for Under 13s). The grass on the pitch is closely mown and rolled flat. Just to make things confusing, sometimes the whole ground is called a 'cricket pitch'.
square	The area in the centre of the ground where the strips are.
strip	Another name for the pitch. They are called strips because there are several pitches side by side on the square. A different one is used for each match.
track	Another name for the pitch or strip.
wicket	'Wicket' means two things, so it can sometimes confuse people. 1 The stumps and bails at each end of the pitch. The batsman defends his wicket. 2 The pitch itself. So you can talk about a hard wicket or a turning wicket (if it's taking spin).

BATTING

attacking strokes	The attacking strokes in cricket all have names. There are forward strokes (played off the front foot) and backward strokes (played

142

off the back foot). **The drawing shows where the different strokes are played around the wicket.**

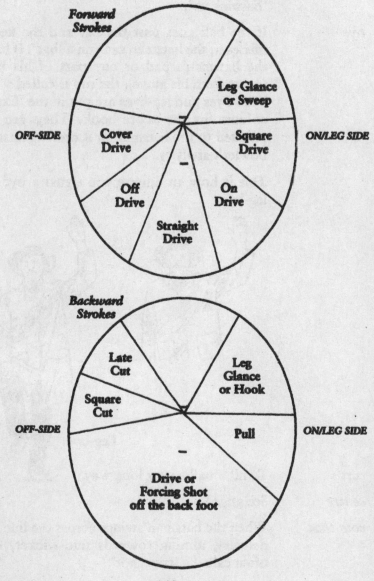

Forward Strokes

Leg Glance or Sweep

Cover Drive

Square Drive

OFF-SIDE

ON/LEG SIDE

Off Drive

On Drive

Straight Drive

Backward Strokes

Late Cut

Leg Glance or Hook

Square Cut

OFF-SIDE

Pull

ON/LEG SIDE

Drive or Forcing Shot off the back foot

backing up	As the bowler bowls, the non-striking batsman should start moving down the wicket to be ready to run a quick single. This is called 'backing up'.
bye	If the ball goes past the bat and the keeper misses it, the batsmen can run a 'bye'. If it hits the batsman's pad or any part of his body (apart from his glove), the run is called a 'leg-bye'. Byes and leg-byes are put in the 'Extras' column in the score-book. They are not credited to the batsman or scored against the bowler's analysis.

This is how an umpire will signal a bye and leg-bye.

Bye

Leg-bye

cart	To hit a ball a very long way.
centre	See guard
cow shot	When the batsman swings across the line of a delivery, aiming towards mid-wicket, it is often called a 'cow shot'.

144

defensive strokes	There are basically two defensive shots: the 'forward defensive', played off the front foot and the 'backward defensive' played off the back foot.
duck	When a batsman is out before scoring any runs it's called a 'duck'. If he's out first ball for nought it's a 'golden duck'.
gate	If a batsman is bowled after the ball has passed between his bat and pads it is sometimes described as being bowled 'through the gate'.
guard	When you go in to bat the first thing you do is 'take your guard'. You hold your bat sideways in front of the stumps and ask the umpire to give you a guard. He'll show you which way to move the bat until it's in the right position. The usual guards are 'leg stump' (sometimes called 'one leg'); 'middle and leg' ('two leg') and 'centre' or 'middle'.

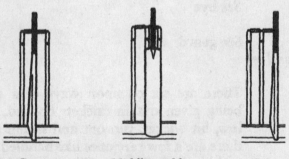

Centre   Middle and leg   Leg

hit wicket	If the batsman knocks off a bail with his bat

or any part of his body when the ball is in play, he is out 'hit wicket'.

innings	This means a batsman's stay at the wicket. 'It was the best *innings* I'd seen Azzie play.' But it can also mean the batting score of the whole team. 'In their first *innings* England scored 360.'
knock	Another word for a batsman's innings.
lbw	Means leg before wicket. In fact a batsman can be given out lbw if the ball hits any part of his body and the umpire thinks it would have hit the stumps. There are two important extra things to remember about lbw: 1 If the ball pitches outside the leg stump and hits the batsman's pads it's not out – even if the ball would have hit the stumps. 2 If the ball pitches outside the off-stump and hits the pad outside the line, it's not out if the batsman is playing a shot. If he's not playing a shot he can still be given out.
leg-bye	See bye
middle/ *middle and leg*	See guard
out	There are six common ways of a batsman being given out in cricket: bowled, caught, lbw, hit wicket, run out and stumped. Then there are a few rare ones like handled the ball and hit the ball twice. When the fielding side thinks the batsman is out they must appeal (usually a shout of 'Owzthat'). If the umpire

considers the batsman is out, he will signal 'out' like this:

play forward/back	You play forward by moving your front foot down the wicket towards the bowler as you play the ball. You play back by putting your weight on the back foot and leaning towards the stumps. You play forward to well-pitched-up bowling and back to short-pitched bowling.
rabbit	Poor or tail-end batsman.
run	A run is scored when the batsman hits the ball and runs the length of the pitch. If he fails to reach the popping crease before the ball is thrown in and the bails are taken off, he is 'run out'. Four runs are scored when the ball is hit across the boundary. Six runs are scored when it crosses the boundary without bouncing. This is how the umpire signals 'four':

This is how the umpire signals 'six':

If the batsman does not put his bat down inside the popping crease at the end of a run before setting off on another run, the umpire will signal 'one short' like this.

A run is then deducted from the total by the scorer.

stance   The stance is the way a batsman stands and holds his bat when he is waiting to receive a delivery. There are many different types of stance. For instance, 'side on', with the shoulder pointing down the wicket; 'square on', with the body turned towards the bowler; 'bat raised' and so on.

striker   The batsman who is receiving the bowling.
                   The batsman at the other end is called the
                   non-striker.

stumped   If you play and miss and the wicket-keeper
                   knocks a bail off with the ball in his hands,
                   you will be out 'stumped' if you are out of
                   your crease.

ton   A century. One hundred runs scored by a bats-
                   man.

BOWLING

arm ball   A variation by the off-spinner (or left-arm
                   spinner) which swings in the air in the oppo-
                   site direction to the normal spin, i.e. away
                   from the right-handed batsman in the case of
                   the off-spinner.

beamer   See full toss.

block hole   A ball bowled at yorker length is said to pitch
                   in the 'block hole' – i.e. the place where the
                   batsman marks his guard and rests his bat on
                   the ground when receiving.

bouncer   The bowler pitches the ball very short and
                   bowls it hard into the ground to get extra
                   bounce and surprise the batsman. The ball
                   will often reach the batsman at shoulder
                   height or above. But you have to be a fast
                   bowler to bowl a good bouncer. A slow
                   bouncer is often called a 'long hop' and is easy
                   to pull or cut for four.

chinaman	A left-arm bowler who bowls with the normal leg-break action will deliver an off-break to the right-handed batsman. This is called a 'chinaman'.
dot ball	A ball from which the batsman does not score a run. It is called this because it goes down as a dot in the score-book.
flipper	A variation on the leg-break. It is bowled from beneath the wrist, squeezed out of the fingers, and it skids off the pitch and goes straight through. It shouldn't be attempted by young cricketers because it puts a lot of strain on the wrist and arm ligaments.
full toss	A ball which doesn't bounce before reaching the batsman is a full toss. Normally it's easy to score off a full toss, so it's considered a bad ball. A high full toss from a fast bowler is called a 'beamer'. It is very dangerous and should never be bowled deliberately.
googly	A 'googly' is an off-break bowled with a leg break action (see **leg break**) out of the back of the hand like this.

grubber	A ball which hardly bounces – it pitches and shoots through very low, usually after hitting a bump or crack in the pitch. Sometimes also called a shooter.
hat trick	Three wickets from three consecutive balls by one bowler. They don't have to be in the same over i.e. two wickets from the last two balls of one over and one from the first of the next.
half-volley	See length
leg break/ off-break	The 'leg break' is a delivery from a spinner which turns from leg to off. An 'off-break' turns from off to leg.
	That's easy to remember when it's a right-hand bowler bowling to a right-hand batsman. But when a right-arm, off-break bowler bowls to a left-handed bat he is bowling leg-breaks. And a left-hander bowling with an off-break action bowls leg-breaks to a right-hander. It takes some working out – but the drawing helps.

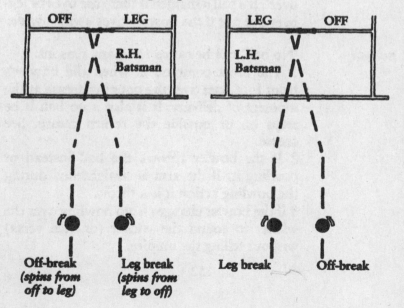

leg-cutter/ *off-cutter*	A ball which cuts away off the pitch from leg to off is a 'leg-cutter'. The 'off-cutter' goes from off to leg. Both these deliveries are bowled by fast or medium-pace bowlers. See seam bowling.
leggie	Slang for a leg-spin bowler.
length	You talk about the 'length' or 'pitch' of a ball bowled. A good length ball is one that makes the batsman unsure whether to play back or forward. A short-of-a-length ball pitches slightly closer to the bowler than a good length. A very short-pitched ball is called a 'long hop'. A 'half-volley' is an over-pitched ball which bounces just in front of the batsman and is easy to drive.
long hop	A ball which pitches very short. See length.
maiden over	If a bowler bowls an over without a single run being scored off the bat, it's called a 'maiden over'. It's still a maiden if there are byes or leg-byes but not if the bowler gives away a wide.
no ball	'No ball' can be called for many reasons. 1 The most common is when the bowler's front foot goes over the popping crease at the moment of delivery. It is also a no ball if he steps on or outside the return crease. See crease. 2 If the bowler throws the ball instead of bowling it. If the arm is straightened during the bowling action it is a throw. 3 If the bowler changes from bowling over the wicket to round the wicket (or vice versa) without telling the umpire.

4 If there are more than two fielders behind square on the leg side. (There are other fielding regulations with the limited overs game. For instance, the number of players who have to be within the circle.)

A batsman can't be out off a no ball, except run out. A penalty of one run (an experiment of two runs is being tried in county cricket) is added to the score and an extra ball must be bowled in the over. The umpire shouts 'no ball' and signals like this:

over the wicket   If a right-arm bowler delivers the ball from the right of the stumps (as seen by the batsman) i.e. with his bowling arm closest to the stumps, then he is bowling 'over the wicket'. If he bowls from the other side of the stumps he is bowling 'round the wicket'.

pace   The pace of the ball is the speed it is bowled at. A fast or pace bowler like Waqar Younis can bowl at speeds of up to 90 miles an hour. The different speeds of bowlers range from fast through medium to slow with in-between speeds like fast-medium and medium-fast (fast-medium is the faster).

153

pitch	See **length**.
round the wicket	See **over the wicket**
seam	The seam is the sewn, raised ridge which runs round a cricket ball.
seam bowling	Bowling – usually medium to fast – where the ball cuts into or away from the batsman off the seam.
shooter	See *grubber*.
spell	A 'spell' of bowling is the number of overs bowled in succession by a bowler. So if a bowler bowls six overs before being replaced by another bowler, he has bowled a spell of six overs.
swing bowling	A cricket ball can be bowled to swing through the air. It has to be bowled in a particular way to achieve this and one side of the ball must be polished and shiny. Which is why you always see fast bowlers shining the ball. An 'in-swinger' swings into the batsman's legs from the off-side. An 'out-swinger' swings away towards the slips.
trundler	A steady, medium-pace bowler who is not particularly good.
turn	Another word for spin. You can say 'the ball turned a long way' or 'it spun a long way'.
wicket maiden	An over when no run is scored off the bat and the bowler takes one wicket or more.

wide   If the ball is bowled too far down the leg side
or the off-side for the batsman to reach (usually the edge of the return crease is the line
umpires look for) it is called a 'wide'. One run
is added to the score and an extra ball is
bowled in the over.

In limited overs cricket wides are given for
balls closer to the stumps – any ball bowled
down the leg side risks being called a wide in
this sort of 'one-day' cricket.

This is how an umpire signals a wide.

yorker   A ball, usually a fast one – bowled to bounce
precisely under the batsman's bat. The most
dangerous yorker is fired in fast towards the
batsman's legs to hit leg stump.

FIELDING

backing up   A fielder backs up a throw to the wicket-
keeper or bowler by making sure it doesn't go
for overthrows. So when a throw comes in to
the keeper, a fielder is positioned behind him
to cover him if he misses it. Not to be confused
with a *batsman* backing up.

chance   A catchable ball. So to miss a chance is the
same as to drop a catch.

close/deep	Fielders are either placed close to the wicket (near the batsman) or in the deep or 'out-field' (near the boundary).
cow corner	The area between the deep mid-wicket and long-on boundaries where a *cow shot* is hit to.
dolly	An easy catch.
hole-out	A slang expression for a batsman being caught. 'He holed out at mid-on.'
overthrow	If the ball is thrown to the keeper or the bowler's end and is misfielded allowing the batsmen to take extra runs, these are called 'overthrows'.
silly	A fielding position very close to the batsman and in front of the wicket e.g. silly mid-on.
sledging	Using abusive language and swearing at a batsman to put him off. A slang expression – first used in Australia.
square	Fielders 'square' of the wicket are on a line with the batsman on either side of the wicket. If they are fielding further back from this line, they are 'behind square' or 'backward of square'; if they are fielding in front of the line i.e. closer to the bowler, they are 'in front of square' or 'forward of square'.
standing up/ standing back	The wicket-keeper 'stands up' to the stumps for slow bowlers. This means he takes his

position immediately behind the stumps. For fast bowlers he stands well back – often several yards away for very quick bowlers. He may either stand up or back for medium-pace bowlers.

GENERAL WORDS

colts County Colts teams are selected from the best young cricketers in the county at all ages from Under 11 to Under 17. Junior league cricket is usually run by the County Colts Association.

under 11s/ 12s etc. You qualify for an Under 11 team if you are 11 or under on September 1st prior to the cricket season. So if you're 12 but you were 11 on September 1st last year, you can play for the Under 11s.

————————— • —————————

FIELDING POSITIONS

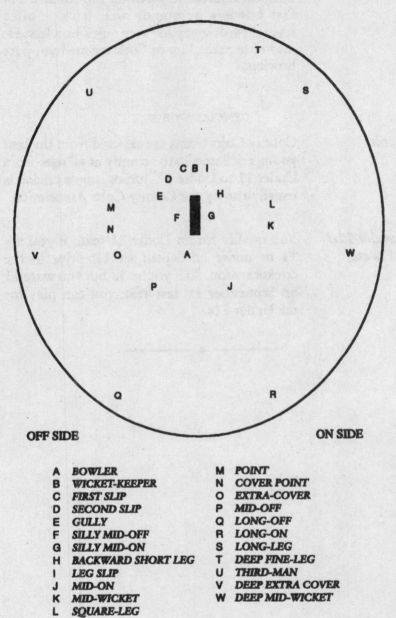

OFF SIDE

ON SIDE

A	*BOWLER*	M	*POINT*
B	*WICKET-KEEPER*	N	*COVER POINT*
C	*FIRST SLIP*	O	*EXTRA-COVER*
D	*SECOND SLIP*	P	*MID-OFF*
E	*GULLY*	Q	*LONG-OFF*
F	*SILLY MID-OFF*	R	*LONG-ON*
G	*SILLY MID-ON*	S	*LONG-LEG*
H	*BACKWARD SHORT LEG*	T	*DEEP FINE-LEG*
I	*LEG SLIP*	U	*THIRD-MAN*
J	*MID-ON*	V	*DEEP EXTRA COVER*
K	*MID-WICKET*	W	*DEEP MID-WICKET*
L	*SQUARE-LEG*		

GLORY IN THE CUP

BOB CATTELL

Hooker, Azzie, Erica and the rest all play cricket in their spare time, but they've never taken it very seriously until now. Kiddo, one of their school teachers, suggests they form an official team and play proper matches – and Glory Gardens C.C. is formed. Hooker, as captain, soon finds out that cricket teams weren't built in a day: some players squabble, some can't catch, and some have tantrums and go home at half-time! So will Glory Gardens go all out for victory . . . or will they be out for a duck?

ISBN – 978 0 099 46111 1
RED FOX
£4.99

GLORY
GARDENS
CRICKET CLUB

BOUND
FOR GLORY

BOB CATTELL

Glory Gardens C.C. is now in the North County
Under Thirteen League, and the pressure is really on.
Hooker, as captain, worries that the team won't be able
to hold it together: arrogant Clive is always picking fights,
Ohbert is still as useless as ever, and there are all the usual
rows and injuries. But there's also Mack, the new player;
the lucky mascot, 'Gatting'; plus the whole team's
unwavering determination to win against
all the odds.

ISBN – 978 0 099 46121 0
RED FOX
£4.99